I0546222

lf the Curse Fits

A Hex on Me Mystery
Book One

KENNEDY LAYNE

IF THE CURSE FITS

Copyright © 2019 by Kennedy Layne
Print Edition

eBook ISBN: 978-1-943420-75-9
Print ISBN: 978-1-943420-76-6

Cover Designer: Sweet 'N Spicy Designs

ALL RIGHTS RESERVED: The unauthorized reproduction or distribution of this copyrighted work is illegal. Criminal copyright infringement is investigated by the FBI and is punishable by up to 5 years in federal prison and a fine of $250,000.

All characters and events in this book are fictitious. Any resemblance to actual persons living or dead is strictly coincidental.

DEDICATION

Jeffrey—In our story, it would be "If the Love Fits"…and it certainly does!

Cole—Always remember…you can succeed in anything with enough determination.

USA Today Bestselling Author Kennedy Layne brings a completely different twist to her brand new cozy paranormal mystery series that you won't want to miss!

Have you ever heard of a cursed witch? Well, that's exactly what Tempest "Lou" Lilura has become, and she's willing to do just about anything to rectify her desperate situation. Unfortunately, the consequences of being hexed by the only immortal Lich Queen has kept Lou a little too busy to find a solution to her problem.

What's the hex, you ask? In Lou's tragic case, her curse gives her the foresight of murders yet to be committed. It's the ultimate race against time—can she discover the culprit prior to the actual deed or can she save the victim and catch the murderer in the act?

This poor hexed witch is going to going to need all the help she can get. Unfortunately, her help comes in the form of a warlock who is obsessed with conspiracy theories, an overly optimistic yet naïve healer, and a rather pretentious familiar who has an obsession for proper etiquette. Come join this traveling mystery band while they try to solve another murder as they're faced with powerful druids, two odd magical hares, and a mysterious man who definitely knows more than he's willing to saying.

Chapter One

"I BET YOU'VE never heard this one before—a cursed witch."

I usually loved the initial reaction I received upon someone hearing of my unique paradox. Unfortunately, I didn't experience any satisfaction when the petite blonde barista handed me the black coffee I'd ordered without a second glance.

I mean, she didn't even seem to blink twice.

It had me wondering if she'd heard me at all. She'd literally had absolutely no outward reaction.

"Piper, I know what you are," I murmured, attempting once more to entice any type of response at this point. "Can you please take a break so that you can hear me out?"

Of course, I'd kept my voice low so that none of the other patrons could hear our one-sided conversation. It wouldn't do to have someone inadvertently hear me talking about the supernatural as if it were more than a television show for teenagers to drone on about in between their high school classes.

Nothing I did seemed to matter, though.

I got nothing from her.

Piper set another to-go cup underneath a spout that began dispensing hot milk as if I'd already walked away from the counter. I struggled to garner her attention one more time with a genuine desperate plea.

"I really need your help."

Trust me, I wasn't beneath begging at this point.

I'd basically been forced into a corner.

"I'm sorry, but I have no idea what you're talking about," Piper replied with a look of innocence I'd never quite been able to master. She even went so far as to give me a small apologetic smile as she continued working the machine in front of her, causing steam to billow up from one of the hot beverages she'd gone back to concocting. She'd beat me at my own game. The shock value of my public approach only left me wondering about my tactics. I wasn't going to be able to stand in front of the pickup counter for much longer without someone noticing that I'd already received my drink and been dismissed. "You must have me confused with someone else. You'll have to excuse me. I'm working here."

Well, so much for my offensive strategy.

I had no choice but to walk over to the side counter that contained the various types of sweeteners and creamers after Piper had called out another customer's name. She'd essentially snubbed me, and there wasn't a thing I could do about her obvious brushoff.

It didn't take me long to add two packets of sugar and a short pour of half and half into my coffee. I then stirred the mystical ingredients together before walking over to where my other recruit sat at a small table in the back corner with his mass of electronic gadgets plugged into practically all the nearby outlets.

Recruit might have been a bit of an exaggeration.

Okay, it was a total embellishment.

To put it bluntly, I was paying Orwin Cornelia a rather hefty amount of cash to help me with my current—and for the foreseeable future—hugely colossal problem that had been bestowed upon my most unlucky self.

Don't get me wrong.

He did have a slight personal stake in my dilemma, but that was something we didn't talk about…ever.

"Did she say yes?" Orwin asked, using his index finger to push up the black-rimmed glasses that had a tendency to constantly slip down the bridge of his nose. His dark gaze had been hopping around to all the different customers like a caffeinated jumping bean ever since we'd entered the quaint little coffee shop. "Did she even respond? She didn't, did she? Can we go now? I told you this would happen."

"No, Orwin, we can't go," I replied softly, wishing I could cast a calming spell over him to keep him from acting so suspiciously odd. Given that he was one of the best wizards of his generation and that he'd seen what had happened to me firsthand, he'd made it virtually impossible for anyone to do the same to him. Trust me, that type of spell hadn't been easy to pull off. If only I'd been that smart to begin with, I wouldn't be in this totally unbelievable and completely unjustified dire situation. "Piper Allifair won't give me the time of day…yet. We can't leave here without her help, though. It's just another brick wall before us that we'll figure out how to go around, climb over, or dig under."

There was nothing I could do about Orwin's apprehension, but he'd be the first one to notice if something was amiss in our current surroundings. He was a bit of a conspiracy theorist, and his situational awareness was now dialed up to a ten plus. You know, aliens and such. I'd have thought dealing with the supernatural was enough, but he apparently liked to take things a bit further down that road to crazy town.

It wasn't that I expected anything else to happen. Today had been quiet given some of the more recent events we'd had to deal with. I guess in the grand scheme of things, what's worse than being cursed by an immortal Lich?

In case you weren't familiar with the meaning of the word Lich, it was basically an ultra-powerful undead witch or warlock whose powers were so transcendent that they became immune to the grasp of death. Liches bound their intellect and what was left of their souls, as they were known to exist, to a physical object known as a phylactery or magical amulet.

Interesting tidbit, huh?

Not even death could claim them, which was where their form of immortality came into the picture. Their physical form suffered the normal degradations of the dead; however, most of those exceedingly rare creatures were known to disguise their outward appearance so that they could move about freely and without notice.

Not that I'd ever witnessed such a thing myself, but the old witch's tales believed that Liches tended to disintegrate into skeletal figures after a couple hundred years. It was even said that their flesh fell off their undead bodies once they tired of dragging their corpse around the mortal world.

"Death."

"What?"

Orwin had definitely caught my attention.

"You asked what was worse than being cursed by an immortal Lich." Orwin shrugged as if the answer was obvious. "Death."

I shot Orwin an agitated glance as I sipped my coffee, loathing the fact that he could read my thoughts as if I'd spelled them all out for him in my diary. As I'd mentioned before, he was one of the most talented wizards at the extremely young age of twenty-one. Most wizards needed decades of study to perfect their art. Unfortunately, his mindreading skills unconsciously came into play when someone was within six feet of him.

I purposefully scooted back my chair, but it wasn't nearly far enough to be outside of his extrasensory gift's area of effect.

"Curse would be more accurate. Gift would imply someone else's opinion…wrong as they might be."

"Would you stop that," I snapped, irritated that he couldn't shut off his annoying habit. That didn't mean it couldn't come in handy, especially in a circumstance like this. "Orwin, why don't you go and order yourself a cup of coffee? Actually, make that a nice green tea. It should calm your nerves. See if Piper is showing any curiosity at all to my unsolicited plea of help."

I reached into the pocket of my favorite black leather jacket and handed Orwin a five-dollar bill. After all, I was technically his employer and this was a work assignment. He arched a thin black eyebrow at the money in my hand.

"Then I need a raise," Orwin declared with a frown, snatching the green piece of currency out of my fingers. He took a fortifying breath before standing from his chair. "And a new laptop. Oh, and preferably one with a one terabyte solid state drive and a decent clock speed."

"I just bought you a new one three months ago," I complained, but he was already out of earshot and…mindshot? That probably wasn't even a word, but I'd go with it for the time being.

I sat back in my seat while keeping an eye on Piper and our overall surroundings, wondering what it would take to get her to listen to my plight. She'd never once paused in her task as a barista, and she continued to smile at each patron who gathered their post-workday sample of liquid sanity in a cup.

Had I made a mistake?

Had Piper not come into her power at a young age like us?

It wasn't unheard of, but that would mean I'd come all this way for nothing but disappointment.

No, I couldn't doubt myself or Orwin's research. Piper Allifair was definitely a witch, of that I was certain.

Orwin and I had spent a great deal of time searching for someone in the Allifair family line who could do what the great Warlock Allifair had done back in his time—heal a witch with the simple touch of his hand. Such powers were normally reserved for arch druids or priests of immense power.

It stood to reason there was a chance the Allifair gift could dispel the hateful magic created by a curse. Their family lineage contained such an amazing and rare talent, and I needed all the help I could get in lifting this wicked jinx that had been bestowed upon me for simply being in the wrong place at the wrong time.

I might have been a little bit on edge, as a round of laughter that rose from a nearby table had me startling just a bit.

Four young women had been sitting a couple feet away ever since Orwin and I had walked into the café.

One of them had disappeared, probably to the restroom, leaving three behind to say a few things that told me the fourth wasn't well-liked—and that explained why they had foregone the time-honored need to use the facilities in pairs.

What was so wrong with this world that people couldn't even be nice to one another anymore?

I'd rather know who my enemies were than have fair-weathered friends like that.

On second thought, I'd rather have no enemies at all, given the fact that the current one at the top of the list had powers and abilities that were completely beyond my reach and capability to conceptualize.

I sighed impatiently, noting from the clock hanging on the back wall that it was going on seven o'clock in the evening. Most of the patrons had placed their orders before quickly leaving with their drinks in hand. They were undoubtedly headed home to wind down from their day.

Orwin had wanted to come back later, claiming this wasn't the time or place to corner Piper with our offer. He'd thought we should wait until closing time. Maybe he'd been right, but I wasn't one to waste precious time.

Full disclosure—I wasn't the most patient person in the world.

I had once had the world by the tail and longed to be there once again so that I was in control of my own destiny.

Besides, allowing Piper to think things over while mindlessly completing the task of making lattes wasn't such a bad thing. The shock of my admission would most likely have worn off by the time she was ready to sit down and talk with us later.

I was completely prepared, and I had my speech all laid out as to why she should help.

I'd tell her that my name was Tempest Lilura—Lou to my friends—and that I'd been cursed by the queen of all Liches for simply being in the wrong place at the wrong time. I was completely innocent of any wrongdoing and blamelessly cursed for only my proximity to the real culprit.

It wouldn't take long after that to explain to Piper that I was here to seek her help to rid me of the resulting hex. If her gift didn't extend to the hexes of all hexes, the next phase of the plan would be to have her join my little team to either hunt down the Lich in question or to find a cure to rid me of this curse.

Simple, right?

I did another scan of my surroundings, something I'd grown used to doing in the last three months. Trust me, you'd have that tendency too if you'd been hexed. I didn't like corners, shadows, or basically not knowing what was headed my way without a bit of forewarning.

Nothing seemed amiss, though.

A man sitting next to another outlet was staring at his computer as if he were hypnotized, two college-aged girls were studying in one of the few booths available, and an older couple was reading the evening paper at a table near the door. Nothing out of the ordinary indicated that this night couldn't end on a good note.

Apparently, I spoke too soon.

I barely caught my coffee before it fell off the table. No magic involved, either.

Someone had bumped into my elbow, most likely coming back from the restrooms down the small hall. The man immediately muttered an apology, complained about a cat, and made his way to an empty table where a drink and a backpack had been left to save his spot.

Well, wasn't he a trustworthy soul?

In most larger cities, his backpack and possibly his drink would be highjacked by now.

I vaguely remembered the man being in front of me while I'd been standing in line, but I'd thought he'd left the café. I didn't think it was possible to be rusty in the three days it had been since our last case, but I guess I was mortal, after all.

I'd like it to be known that my interest in the man had nothing to do with the fact that he was roguishly handsome. His short-cropped hair was as black as mine, his chiseled features gave him an air of dominance, and the five o'clock shadow gave him a mysterious vibe. Oh, and the brown leather jacket he was wearing couldn't hide that he kept himself in fine shape. Cut was the term I would use.

No, his looks weren't the reason he'd caught my attention. It was that he had the appearance of an apex predator, *and* the fact that I could have sworn I'd seen him before.

"Knox Emeric." Orwin had returned with what looked like hot chocolate, having completely ignored my suggestion of tea. He reclaimed his seat, but I clearly didn't have his full attention. "He was at the gas station we stopped at right before pulling into town. He didn't like the gas prices. They were more expensive than his previous stop. He's just a harmless fellow traveler."

I loved it when Orwin provided me with information without the need to lift a finger. It didn't sound like he'd picked up on anything about Knox Emeric for me to worry about, so I tore my gaze away from the stranger to focus on what Orwin found so interesting, and it wasn't as remarkable as I would have imagined.

What in the world was a domestic white short-haired cat doing in a café?

I'd heard of those cat cafés that were taking over the Midwest, but I hadn't seen any sign to indicate this was one of them. Considering that Orwin was allergic to basically anything with fur might have had him staying outside in my Jeep. He tried his best to stay away from anyplace that had animals in close quarters to humans.

"She really doesn't like you, does she?" Orwin asked, clearly referring to the sleek white cat that was the apparent reason for Mr. Emeric's apparent stumble.

"Look at the way that cat is glaring at you with those green eyes of hers. Did you step on her tail or something? It's almost like—"

Orwin stopped talking when he attempted to fend off a sneeze.

He wasn't successful.

Three sneezes later, I was holding out a napkin from the dispenser.

"She must belong to someone who works here."

I cautiously kept an eye on the feline, wary that the cat might try to sink her claws into my leg or something. The last thing I needed was to get cat scratch fever or anything of that nature. She just sat there, twitching her tail in an obvious show of displeasure. I wasn't paranoid, like Orwin had the tendency to be, but I was cautious considering my situation.

"I'm sure if we ignore her that she'll go back to doing whatever it was she was doing before we got here," I said, though my words didn't sound as convincing as I'd wanted them to. I waved my hand in her direction. "Shoo."

The white feline was definitely a female. Normally, toms were bulkier and larger through the chest. They exuded a rather scruffy masculine look, where a female tended to be more refined. I did find it odd that her fur was completely devoid of even one speck of dirt. She was obviously a well-kept cat, though clearly not happy that she was surrounded by strangers whom she didn't care for.

"Well, what did you hear while you were up at the counter?" I asked after the cat decided that it was going to sit where she was for the remainder of our stay. I'd read somewhere that cats could be rather obstinate. We didn't have time to concern ourselves with the animal, though. "Is Piper considering sitting down with us to hear more about my curse?"

Who wouldn't want to hear my story? It wasn't every day that a witch was hexed by an immortal. Had this situation not been about me, I would have been the first to pull up a chair at the table.

"Not exactly," Orwin hedged before blowing his nose. I wrinkled mine when he crumbled up the napkin and shoved it in his pocket. Yuck. "Piper is currently trying to figure out when she can take a quick break to call her father."

"Seriously? She's twenty-two years old. It's not like I threatened her or anything."

One of the three women stood up from their table and began walking in our direction. No doubt she was seeing what was taking their friend so long in the restroom. If my friends were backstabbers like these ladies, I wouldn't have stuck around, either. One of the women collected her purse with a frown on her face, and I wasn't so sure she'd still be at the table when the other two came out of the restroom.

"You told Piper about the curse, and then you mentioned her...gift." Orwin had also seen the woman approaching the table, so he leaned in a bit closer so she couldn't hear him. "It stands to reason she thinks you're some hedge witch who heard of her family name and is looking to clear up some acne or something. I'm sure she just wants some advice and some protection for when her shift ends."

Orwin might have been right about waiting to speak with Piper until after her shift. That wasn't for another three hours, though. I couldn't help but run a hand over my jawline, making sure my skin was still as smooth as it was this morning. I had been blessed with porcelain skin, but that meant the slightest blemish could be seen like a beacon. Where did he come up with this acne stuff? I'd grown out of that hormonal stage in my late teens.

"Uh, Lou?" Orwin had gone through another napkin, leaving the sides of his nose looking rather irritated. The expression on his face told me that I shouldn't be worried about his allergies. His wide gaze was currently focused on the door to the women's restroom. "We might have a   "

A muffled bloodcurdling scream could be heard from inside the restroom, but it didn't remain muted for long. The woman who'd just walked past our table came running out in a panic, yelling for someone to call 911. Her words were rather incoherent, but I did pick up on *stabbed* and *dead*.

"Did she just say that her friend was stabbed?" I reiterated, because what were the odds of this happening? Maybe my bad luck didn't just extend to my hex. Oh, I had a bad feeling about this. "Please tell me I heard her wrong."

"I wish I could," Orwin muttered, scooting back his chair quickly as everyone in the café began to react to the hysterics. "But there's definitely been a murder."

Multiple things happened at once.

The white cat arched her back and hissed loudly before running behind the counter. The cashier and the three patrons in line all froze in shock. The young man on the computer was grappling for his phone and most likely trying to record the mania, while the older couple appeared ready to bolt. As for the college girls, they were watching everyone else, clearly attempting to see if this was some kind of prank.

Crud.

This was really happening.

For once, my hex hadn't played a part in this mystery. Unfortunately, there was no leaving this café with a dead body in the restroom. It was then that I saw a blur of a blonde girl go running for the small hallway.

"Piper is going to sneak into the restroom to try and save or revive the victim," I muttered as I quickly stood up from my chair, already hearing a rich, commanding voice talking to a 911 operator. Apparently, Knox

Emeric wasn't one to ignore a crisis. "Oliver, don't let anyone leave this café. It stands to reason that someone inside this place is a murderer."

Chapter Two

"PIPER, YOU DID all you could," I consoled, understanding full well that platitudes like the one I'd just given her didn't make anything better. This wasn't how I'd pictured having a conversation with her, but these past three months had taught me that hardly anything ever went as planned. "We now have to leave this in the hands of the police. They have a job to do here, and we shouldn't get in the way."

It was hard to miss the way Orwin's thin black eyebrow arched above his glasses. He knew me well enough that I wouldn't allow a little thing like a police presence to prevent me from doing a bit of my own sleuthing. He also probably didn't agree with me about my outlook and told me often enough that I was far too obstinate for my own good.

I liked to view myself as determined rather than stubborn.

Anyway, I had no choice but to take advantage of the time I had with Piper.

Unfortunately, the blonde barista *had* tried to save

the victim, but the woman had been dead for at least a minute or two before she'd been discovered. It wasn't like Piper's ability extended to bringing back the dead, when the heart quit beating and the spirit had fled the body. Her abilities had limitations just like everyone else.

I'll spare you the gory details of her desperate attempt to heal a woman who was beyond saving.

What I should share with you was that the town of Bedford was fairly small. Thankfully, it hadn't taken the local police long to show up at the café. As for Orwin, he'd done a great job of keeping everyone inside until the authorities arrived, and the police had made each and every one of us sit at the tables farthest away from the restrooms until they could get everyone's statements.

I'd made sure that Orwin and I had claimed a table with Piper, leaving the other witnesses to gather round a few of the others nearby. Everyone was whispering to one another, probably all wondering who could have committed the vicious murder and speculating if the killer was someone sitting next to them.

"This is all your fault," Piper whispered accusingly, cautiously looking around to see if anyone nearby had overheard her. She brushed a blonde curl away from her face so that I wouldn't miss her accusing glare. It was hard to take her seriously, though. "Nothing this crazy ever happens here. You come along, claiming to be a cursed witch of all things, and now a woman is suddenly dead. What did you do? Transfer your curse to her or something?"

As if right on cue, the white cat Orwin and I had seen earlier jumped up in Piper's lap as if she'd wanted to console the younger woman. I take that back. The feline was definitely defending her owner, especially after the hiss she'd given me.

I'd never imagined that Piper would have a familiar, but now I completely understood why the cat didn't like me.

Okay, it was clear that she loathed me on sight.

I tried to be a bit more understanding. After all, a familiar's love *was* unconditional. This pretty white familiar had been trying to protect her witch, and she undeniably considered me a threat.

The thing of it was…the familiar wasn't wrong if you thought about the sole reason I was here.

"We had nothing to do with that woman's murder," Orwin denied, attempting to scoot back from the dander shedding feline. It was too late, and even I could see the silky white hairs floating in the air between them. He'd somehow managed to keep himself from sneezing…just barely. He shrugged, as if I should have known the answer. "I had some of my allergy medicine left in my pocket."

Oh, that's right.

Orwin and I had encountered a couple of werewolves on our last case. What everyday humans referred to as pet dander extended to the mystical beings of the netherworld. Ever since our encounter with the hairy beasts, he'd carried around his allergy medicine just in case of an emergency. One thing about Orwin I could appreciate was his need to be prepared.

I guess he was a bit of a Boy Scout at heart.

"You've managed to get me where you've wanted me this entire time," Piper pointed out, clearly not happy that I'd cornered her at a table. It was easy to see the mixture of fear and dismay in her blue eyes, and I tried to relax a little to give off the air of tranquility. "The second I give my statement to the police, I'm heading home. You have until then to tell me whatever it is you've come to talk to me about. Is this about his allergies? Tell me that you didn't seek me out to heal his stuffed-up nose."

I went back over our conversation, and it wasn't odd that Piper hadn't quite followed the exchange between me and Orwin. Piper had no idea that Orwin could read minds, not that he was showing any indication that he was doing so now. Maybe he just didn't want to be judged unfairly for a talent he couldn't control.

A quick scan across the café assured me that the police were still busy currently taking Knox Emeric's statement. I found it rather suspicious that he'd wanted to go first, especially considering he'd been in the men's restroom seconds before the victim's body had been found.

Had he snuck into the women's restroom to kill the

victim?

Was Knox Emeric the killer or just a hapless traveler like Orwin had suggested earlier?

We definitely had a finite pool of suspects, and this murder could be solved before midnight if we played our cards right.

"Fine," Orwin sighed, glaring at the ball of white fur curled up in Piper's lap. "I could do with some space from Snowball, there."

Snowball lifted her head and bared her teeth with another drawn-out hiss, letting Orwin know that the dislike was mutual. He didn't waste time scooting back his chair, grabbing a handful of cheap paper napkins, and making haste before joining some of the other witnesses. They were currently all keeping busy by pouring the coffee from the carafes into disposable cups that Piper's fellow workers had put out for the use of the patrons, free of charge.

We had a routine between us that usually worked to our advantage. Orwin would garner what information he could from the gathered crowd, attempting to utilize his gift of telepathy to help find the murderer. I would then discreetly use my power of telekinesis to trap them until the police could arrest them. I know there were more than a few holes in that strategy, but trust me…I'd say that Orwin and I made it work out more than half of the time.

"My familiar's name is Pearl, and she's not beneath

using her claws to make her point," Piper warned, though as I said earlier, it was hard to take the blonde's threat seriously when I was probably five inches taller than her and didn't find her cat frightening in the least. Piper's petite stature made her appear vulnerable, which would motivate almost anyone to want to protect her. With that said, there was an underlying strength that practically emanated from the young girl. "Go on. What is it that you want from me?"

Piper and Pearl.

Go figure.

While I did admire Piper's spunk, Pearl's demeanor left a lot to be desired. A witch or warlock usually acquired a familiar on her or his eighteenth birthday, if she or he was so inclined to attract one. I'd left my coven before my birthday, and Orwin had been seventeen when he'd decided to move on to college. We'd both parted from our families for different reasons, and neither one of us ever had the opportunity to cast the spell nor allow for a familiar to take this dangerous excursion with us.

I guess we could now, given that our circumstances have changed. It was just something we hadn't even considered, in part due to Orwin's allergies. Even witches and warlocks had everyday hurdles to overcome.

I was confused about something, though.

I'd always been told that *all* witches and warlocks could hear a familiar's thoughts. It wasn't supposed to matter who they belonged to, but obviously that wasn't the case here.

Unless Pearl was defective in some manner.

It could be that she just didn't want to communicate with anyone other than her charge.

I couldn't worry about the cat's issues, at the moment. It was best I didn't waste any more time.

"Piper, my name is Tempest Lilura, and I'm the oldest daughter to Cenawin and Dorothea Lilura from a coven in Salem, Massachusetts. I usually go by Lou to my friends, but it's been three months since I've had any of those," I said, hoping that a little injection of humor would get Piper to relax a little. I wasn't sure it was working, so I followed up with another quip. "Unless you count Orwin, but I'm paying him a lot of money to accompany me on this quest."

Needless to say, Piper and Pearl just continued to glare at me as if I was the sole reason they were stuck inside the café with a dead body in the restroom.

Talk about a difficult crowd.

"I don't need to know your name." Piper leaned back in her chair with a clear sigh of frustration and began stroking Pearl behind the ear. "I'll ask again. What is it you want from me? Is it to fix your friend's allergies?"

"Not exactly," I declared reluctantly, having truly wanted this conversation to be a bit friendlier than its current course. So be it. I'd have to lay it all on the line, but I did make a mental note to see if Piper could rid Orwin of his allergies. At least one of us could benefit from this meeting. "I'll be blunt. Ammeline Letty Romilda put a hex on me, and I need your help."

There.

I'd said it aloud.

It wasn't surprising that Piper's pink lips formed the perfect O.

At least now I had her attention.

And mine.

I whipped around, instantly placing my right hand over my ear. It was as if someone had been standing right beside my chair with their lips attached to my earlobe. What a horrible sensation. Icky, in every sense of the word.

"That's just Pearl. She's a bit…finicky…on who she chooses to speak with, and you aren't exactly her favorite person at the moment." Piper leaned forward, much to Pearl's dismay, causing the white feline to sit in Piper's lap instead of being curled up in a ball. It was good to see that Piper was very interested in what I had to say now. "Ammeline Letty Romilda? I thought she was just a legend made up to scare little children when they didn't want to behave properly."

Didn't we all?

"And what kind of hex are you talking about? Do you only have months to live? Are you going to grow old in a matter of days?" Piper's head was moving side to side in her disbelief, her blond curls rocking back and forth. "Ammeline Letty Romilda. Wow, that's quite a story."

Piper wasn't the one having a problem believing what she was hearing. I was still rubbing my ear, trying to get over the fact that I could understand Pearl.

Every.

Word.

Her haughty tone reminded me of one of those fancy British ladies who'd been born into royalty. Either that or someone off the Great British Baking show on television.

Haughty, am I? At least I'm not the one who is claiming to be hexed by the bogeyman, Miss Lilura.

"Can Pearl read my thoughts, too?" I asked in suspicion, lowering my hand slowly and wishing this place offered more than coffee. This was not how I'd imagined my talk with Piper panning out. "Forget it. Please tell Pearl not to talk anymore. Now I totally get why Orwin believes his gift is a curse. I would too, if I were in his shoes."

When had my life gone so far off the rails?

I mean, I know the exact moment, but what had I done to warrant such bad karma?

I'm sure there's a list somewhere, Miss Lilura. Your parents might have it in their possession.

Oh, I might have to rethink my proposition to Piper. This part about hearing voices in my head might literally drive me off the deep end.

"The police are about to question Marna and Jack," Piper shared somewhat conspiringly, most likely hoping to distract me from Pearl's not-so-pleasant attitude. "Marna and Jack are new here in town, but they're really very sweet. I can't believe for a second that they had anything to do with that woman's death. And what do you mean, Orwin's *gift* is a curse?"

"Don't let the couple's appearance fool you," I replied, diverting the conversation away from Orwin. I only had so many minutes to state my case, and I for one knew firsthand how looks could be deceiving. "Piper, it doesn't matter what hex Ammeline has cursed me with. What matters most right now is whether you can make it go away."

I instinctively held my breath, wishing more than anything Piper would give me the answer I sought. Orwin and I had disagreed about her abilities many times over the last few weeks after finding out about her existence. He didn't believe that Piper's gift of healing extended to ridding one of curses, especially one bestowed by a Lich. I was hoping he was dead wrong.

"It all depends on the type of hex you're talking about," Piper replied cautiously, unknowingly making Orwin and I both right about her gift. She was still watching the older couple speaking to one of the police officers who'd been relegated to taking statements. It took a moment before her blue eyes finally focused back on me, her astonishment at my predicament not hard to miss. "Ammeline Letty Romilda. She really exists? I can't believe she's real. I mean, she's an honest to goodness

Lich queen from antiquity. Did you know that the mental abilities of the mind of a Lich queen stabilizes once committed to the phylactery object as their body deteriorates, leaving only a leathery corpse in an undead form?"

"Yes, I'm aware," I replied, not really in the mood for a history lesson. There was also the dead body in the restroom that we needed to deal with, which hopefully Orwin was narrowing down the suspects. My bet was still on Knox Emeric. "Piper, all I really need to know is—"

"The power of a Lich will eventually spoil and turn rancid, just as her body does. But only when the amulet or the quality of her receptacle degrades." Piper rested her heart-shaped face into the palm of her hand, making sure she left enough room between her and the table for Pearl. "At least, that's what I was told during story time when I was younger. Ammeline is the only modern one in existence today, that we know of, of course. Even the word *Lich* means *corpse* in Old English."

I'd mentioned before that I didn't have a lot of patience.

Piper was dragging out this conversation when a simple yes or no would have sufficed.

I inhaled deeply, struggling to find some fortitude where I was pretty sure there was none. It seemed that the only way I was going to move this along in the short period of time that we had available to us was to tell my life's story.

"Things went south for me around three months ago, and I mean very far south."

In case you didn't realize it, you are in Pennsylvania, Miss Lilura. I can give you directions, though.

I sat back against my chair, unable to get used to the experience of hearing Pearl. The way she said my proper name was like nails being scraped down a chalkboard.

The feeling is mutual, my dear.

Was it warm in here?

I always got a bit antsy when telling this story, but the heat definitely needed to be turned down somewhat. The police were taking their sweet time getting through the statements—not that I blamed them when there was a dead body lying on the cold tile of the women's restroom—so I might as well get comfortable. It didn't take me long to shed my leather jacket.

Now, where was I?

"I had been living in Seattle, teaching a psychology class to a bunch of freshman at a small community college. In all honesty, my life had been going great—a fantastic job where they'd appreciated my contribution, pretty good pay, and some wonderful friends who'd been totally ignorant of what and who I was." If anyone could understand the importance of hiding our lineage, it was another witch. "One itsy-bitsy mistake changed all that."

Itsy-bitsy? My dear Miss Lilura, one doesn't merely become cursed for an itsy-bitsy mistake.

"Pearl, stop that," Piper whispered in admonishment,

though I doubted her light-hearted censure had done much. Pearl didn't seem like the type to take orders. "Tempest is sharing her story. Don't be so judgmental."

That's hard to do, my sweet Piper. Trouble appears to follow this woman wherever she goes, even here with us now.

I really, really didn't like this familiar thing.

Don't get me wrong.

I loved all animals, but listening to a familiar was like having a fly constantly buzzing in my ear. We obviously didn't like one another, and Pearl wasn't even my familiar. So, it stood to reason we didn't even have to exchange words, and the white-haired hoity-toity princess could keep her comments to herself.

Heavens to Betsy! Why, you—

"My name is Lou," I cleared up, not wanting to hear my given name for the next fifty years. I had good reason for that, but that story was for another time. "You really need to tell Pearl to—"

"We have a problem," Orwin exclaimed, practically sliding into his seat after he tried to scan the other witnesses waiting to be interviewed. He pushed up his black-rimmed glasses while observing the small crowd. "Someone inside this café is blocking my ability to pick up on anyone else's thoughts. Lou, that could only mean one thing."

"What's that?" Piper asked warily, holding on to Pearl a little tighter. At least the young blonde witch had good instincts. "Wait a minute. You can read my thoughts?"

Bollocks! A druid, you say?

Piper and Pearl *should* be scared, but not because of Orwin's abilities.

Orwin and I had encountered many things on the road during the last three months. Some other witches and warlocks, mostly basic humans with nefarious intent, and the rare confrontation with other unusual creatures that went bump in the night.

Bottom line?

There really *were* vampires, werewolves, and ghouls that were better left undisturbed.

Sometimes, like right this minute, that was rather hard to do.

This could be a dog's dinner if the situation is not handled properly, my sweet Piper.

"Piper, it means that there's a druid nearby who is most likely the murderer of that poor woman in the restroom." Orwin then titled his head in confusion, his focus solely on me. "A dog's dinner? Really? And since when did you start thinking in an English accent?"

That would be me speaking, Mr. Cornelia. Pearl Pippa Allifair at your service.

Chapter Three

"**I** NEED TO finish my story," I told Orwin, wanting him to buy me a little more time. He was still staring at Pearl in horror after discovering that she'd practically considered herself royalty, while I was doing my best to scour the expressions of everyone else at the other tables to find the culprit. A druid? That wasn't going to work out good for any of us, and we could find ourselves in a lot of trouble. "Orwin, please give me a few more minutes with Piper. Maybe that will be long enough for you to find the druid so I can somehow drop a clue to the police betraying the fact that we know he or she is the guilty party."

Mr. Cornelia, please stop staring at me as if I were one of those green aliens you hope to discover at Area 51.

"I'm pretty sure this is among my top ten worst fears," Orwin whispered in abstract horror. "No wonder we never conjured our familiars. You'd have ended up with a sloth, and I'd have to explain some mouse in my pocket. This kind of crazy horse pucky is going to send me straight to an asylum. Lou, tell that thing to get out of my head, or I'll have to find a new way to skin a cat."

As if right on cue, Orwin sneezed.

The redness on either side of his nose had begun to gradually fade, but it was now back in full color after using another paper napkin. Clearly, his allergy medicine wasn't quite up to the task when it came to these kinds of close quarters.

I'm not a thing, Mr. Cornelia. You're old enough to know that you should refrain from name calling your superiors.

"Go," I directed Orwin, casting Pearl a look that told her not to say another word. I wasn't positive, but I was relatively sure her right eyebrow lifted in disdain. "Try to find the druid. The faster we leave this place, the better for everyone here."

Druids are spellcasters closely related to the Celtic religious followers. They're talented fighters with magical capabilities better suited for the woodlands.

Bottom line?

They weren't to be messed with.

A druid could drop a lone witch without breaking much of a sweat. That same druid in a forest glade could wipe out a small army with little more than mere effort.

It seems we finally agree on something, Miss Lilura.

"Fine," Orwin finally relented, though his reluctance was obvious. "But tell her to stop. I can't deal with that distraction right now."

I was just grateful to have a little more time with

Piper. I didn't miss that Knox Emeric had moved closer and taken a seat just two tables away, but I could still exchange words with the petite healer without him overhearing us if I spoke in hushed tones.

Unfortunately, I just wasn't so sure where to start.

I can help you with that, Miss Lilura. We were discussing the itsy-bitsy mistake you made in order to cause the horrible Lich queen to put a hex on you.

I'm pretty sure that Pearl misunderstood me on purpose, but there was no use in arguing with her.

I'm glad we're getting off on the right paw.

"The hex Ammeline Letty Romilda put on me is quite complicated," I replied honestly, tensing as I waited for Pearl to put in her two cents. She'd even narrowed her green eyes at my admission, but thankfully, she remained silent. "I was simply in the wrong place at the wrong time."

"What does that even mean?" Piper asked, rubbing the back of her neck when a police officer asked one of the college girls to move over to one of the far tables to speak with him. "You were in the wrong place at the wrong time? And not to get off topic, but I know those girls over there. They wouldn't have had anything to do with something like this…"

Piper let her voice trail off, no doubt due to the return of the horrible memories of her time in the restroom trying to revive a corpse.

"It means that I simply said good morning to an

elderly gentleman brushing past me with a cane in his hand," I replied, not wanting to lose Piper's interest just yet. I know I was coming across as cold and uncaring to what happened to the woman in the restroom, but Piper had the ability to save hundreds—if not thousands—of witches and warlocks. "Piper?"

I find it hard to believe that good manners caused the great Ammeline to curse you for all eternity. It sounds to me like you're leaving out something of significance, Miss Lilura.

On second thought, another cup of coffee sounded pretty good. Seeing as the police were halfway through with statements and it appeared that the body was about ready to be moved by the local medical examiner, I would definitely have settled for something less than wine. Anything at this point to hold something in my hands to prevent me from pushing Pearl off of Piper's lap.

That's not very ladylike behavior, now is it? And in case you hadn't noticed, I was doing my best to get my sweet Piper's mind off the hideous nature of the crime committed right here in her place of employment.

I wasn't sure what to say about the manner in which Pearl had tried to assist me, but it wasn't like I could ignore the lifeline she'd tossed my way.

I don't provide that many, Miss Lilura.

"My story goes like this—I'd stopped into a café similar to this one right before my eight o'clock class. I'd grabbed my usual double shot espresso and a slice of my favorite coffeecake, made my way out through the throng of college students looking for the same general morning pick-me-up, and had immediately begun my short walk across campus, bothering absolutely no one. It was then that I said hello to the elderly man with the cane who appeared in my path."

"I don't mean to follow in Pearl's pawprints, but you obviously bothered Ammeline Letty Romilda in some major way," Piper pointed out, relaxing a bit when the officer chose to interview the second college-aged girl. Orwin had finally made his way over to the three ladies, two of whom were still crying. The woman who'd found the victim, however, appeared somewhat shell-shocked compared to the rest. "What happened after you greeted the man with the cane?"

"I then ran into the most charming elderly woman imaginable…only in outward appearance, though. On the inside? She was rotten to the core and undead to boot. The vilest evil known to exist. It practically singed the tiny hairs on the back of my neck. She parted her thin lips and began to chant an incantation I'd never heard before in the most nasally accented tone…let's just say it had been in that moment that I realized I was in some major trouble."

The language had been arcane and powerful, was it not?

"Yes, it was as if the temple runes had come to life." I'm not sure when I had begun replying to Pearl as if she were Piper, but I didn't want to pause in my story. This recap was causing me to break out into a sweat, and I'd already shed my jacket. It wasn't like I could take off this black turtleneck. "Some of the references I'd only ever seen in the bone rune form and had never heard spoken aloud in my life."

Why would such a powerful Lich use that type of curse on you?

I'm pretty sure that Pearl had just given me an insult, but it wasn't like I had the time to take exception to her taunt.

"I later came to find out that the man had been a young warlock in disguise who'd thought it would be a terrific idea to steal a certain mystical cane from the infamous Ammeline Letty Romilda. Its importance was lost on me, and as well as its capabilities." I can still recall in detail every minute of that morning. It was burned into my memory as if it were carved in stone. "The handle on the cane had been beautifully hand-carved into something I can't quite recall now, even with *True Seeing*."

On purpose, of course. It is the cane that harbors Ammeline Letty Romilda's power. It's her phylactery. It is the repository of her intellect and her soul. As such, it would be considered a magical relic.

"It is?" I asked, storing that piece of information away for later use. Maybe destroying the cane could rid me of this hex. Had that been the young warlock's goal? Had he, too, been cursed? It looked as if I needed to give Pearl credit for such a valuable history lesson. "I knew the cane was important to her, but I had no idea that it contained the magic responsible for her immortality."

One thing you must remember before you take your leave, Miss Lilura—every witch in existence fears Ammeline. She's our bogeyman. She is the only sorceress of her family's coven to have ever figured out how to make herself immortal, and that alone makes her a very powerful Lich. The process has been lost for a thousand years. Not that she is alone. Contrary to popular belief, there are whispers of ancient Lich kings who are much older, hidden away from us all. That does not mean Ammeline is not all-powerful. If you must know, she is bound to her physical existence for all time through that extraordinary cane. You should not have crossed her.

"I didn't cross her," I emphatically denied, hating that a cat could get me this riled up. It was time that I go back to ignoring the white familiar, at least for my mental health. "Piper, I did not intentionally misread the situation. I had no idea that the warlock had stolen her cane, nor did I even realize who she was until she began to speak in the ancient tongue."

Who was I kidding? I'd determined from Orwin's research that Piper had come from a very loving family. She was trusting...too trusting.

Which is why she has me, Miss Lilura.

I didn't like that I was having a private conversation where Piper could only hear half or the fact that Pearl had snagged my attention again. All of this felt wrong on every level.

"Can't your family help you?" Piper asked, her blue eyes regarding me with concern. Her question only confirmed my belief about her naiveté when it came to blind trust. "Surely your family coven is not without its own source of power."

Where did I begin? This conversation had gotten so far off track that I wasn't sure how to guide it back to what was important.

Don't get me wrong.

Family was absolutely essential, and I do come from a very revered family of witches. It's the sole reason I have a hefty trust fund. If I were being honest, my mother and father would be absolutely mortified to discover that I'd been hexed by the one and only immortal Lich queen known to exist.

The coven that my parents served on as council was also very well-known, as it should be. We are talking about Salem, after all. But my parents were not the doting mother and father I would have wished for had I had a choice of parents.

That makes me sound very ungrateful, doesn't it?

Now that you mention it…yes, it does.

"Don't you have a mouse to catch or something?" I muttered, accepting that we were running out of time. We were next up in rotation to be questioned by the police and it wouldn't be long before either Piper or myself were giving our statement. Maybe Orwin could take the bullet on the first one from our group. "Look,

Piper, my parents and I aren't exactly on speaking terms. I haven't had any contact with my mother or father for over eight years, ever since the day I turned eighteen and left my coven. They both stated rather vehemently that I wasn't to return once my broomstick crossed the village boundary."

I can see why. Maybe your misfortune was foreseen.

I bit my tongue and told myself over and over again that I was a better person than one who argued with a cat.

And just so you know, I had actually driven from Salam, Massachusetts to Seattle, Washington in a beat-up old red Jeep Wrangler with a soft top and no regrets whatsoever. I still have my most prized possession, which was currently parked right outside the café. It was my wish that we'd be driving away from this town before midnight.

We are not having an argument, Miss Lilura. I'm simply stating facts.

I wanted so very badly to have Pearl call me Lou, but she'd only refuse...and in turn, cause me even more frustration.

"Piper, this is the bottom line. The only thing I can surmise from those precious few moments when I was standing in front of Ammeline was that she mistakenly thought I'd been some sort of accomplice in the theft of her precious cane or worse...that I'd done nothing to apprehend the culprit. Nothing I said or did on that fateful morning got her to see reason."

"So Ammeline put a curse on you?" Piper asked, no longer looking anywhere but me. I understood her fascination, because I would have been the same way upon hearing such a story. Unfortunately, I was the pitiful subject left to deal with a dreadful hex. "And the man you are with? Is he also cursed in the same way?"

"Orwin?" I asked, not that I should have been surprised by her assumption. "Oh, no. He was just a simple bystander who observed my unfortunate circumstance. The only reason I'd recognized his true identity as a warlock was due to his instant reaction to Ammeline's presence and the words he heard her speak. All the other human college students had walked by without giving the older woman a second glance. Orwin? Not so much."

Let's just say that Orwin's thick Coke-bottle glasses had made it easy to tell that his pupils had enlarged to the size of dimes and his mouth had hung open like he was in the business of catching flies. Oh, and his black-rimmed glasses had nearly fallen off his nose.

That doesn't surprise me. I take it he saw the mark?

Pearl was talking about the one distinguishable feature that had been seared into the minds of all witches and warlocks who'd come after her...the infamous wart on the end of Ammeline's nose. Trust me, that specific horrid characteristic was *not* just a fairy tale.

"Yes, Orwin saw the wart," I confessed, tensing when the police officer had relinquished the second college student. He was now headed our way, until he wasn't. "Oh, Orwin. You're a genius."

Orwin had stood up from one of the tables and all but bumped the officer into the table of the older couple, who were grasping for their now cold coffees.

"Tempest—" Piper had begun, but I was quick to cut her off.

"Lou," I insisted, not able to hear my name without hearing the disappointment in my father's tone. It seemed like everyone and their mother had daddy issues. If I could at least get Piper to call me by my nickname, I'd feel as if I'd won half the battle. "Please, call me Lou."

"Fine," Piper relented in that soft tone of hers that made me realize taking her on the road for future cases might not be such a good idea. "How bad is this curse? Do you only have weeks to live? Months?"

You should know that I will do everything in my power to make sure Piper stays here in Bedford...where she belongs, Miss Lilura.

"It's not like that," I corrected Piper, having gotten more than I bargained for with this familiar. It was apparent that Pearl knew what I was going to say before I said it. That was a very unfair advantage. "You see, I think Ammeline believed I should have somehow realized the man had stolen the cane from her that fateful morning. She became so overwrought with anger that she instantly hexed me with the first thing that came to mind—foreseeing the nature of a crime with evil intent before it happens."

I could tell that I'd lost Piper along the way, and Pearl was once again lifting the right side of her whiskers in disdain.

I tried again.

"I'm not talking just any type of crime...but murder. I see murders before they occur. The most heinous crimes you can imagine."

"You're saying you see the gory details of someone taking their last breath before they die?" Piper's blue eyes widened as the meaning behind my words finally hit home. "And when the victim dies, you're left feeling as if you couldn't save them. Is that what happened today? Oh, my goodness. You poor thing. How horrible. What a wicked hex."

That does sound like a travesty, Miss Lilura, but I'm sorry to tell you that Piper cannot rid you of your hex. You must seek help elsewhere...far, far away from here.

Chapter Four

"THAT GENTLEMAN OVER there was in line with me, and he can inform you that neither I nor my companion were anywhere near the restroom," Orwin said loudly, turning the officer's attention to the three men at another table. He'd succeeded in getting the officer's interest off us for a short bit. "Isn't that right, sir?"

"Listen, I'm sorry that I can't help you," Piper said softly, sitting back in her chair now that the police officer tasked with taking statements had shifted his attention over to the three men. "I did come into the Allifair gift on my eighteenth birthday, but it's not that simple. Like anything else dealing with the arts, learning the various healing spells takes time and practice. Truthfully, I'm not that good at it yet, and I'm definitely not dealing with the more serious ailments—if a hex could be called an ailment."

I will make sure my charge gets plenty of practice right here in Bedford, Miss Lilura. Come back in another fifty years or so…on second thought, sixty is a nice number.

"I don't understand why you would want me to go with you if I can't be of any help." Piper had clearly heard Pearl's rejection to my internal thoughts on the subject, but I was quickly realizing that the familiar might be right. I wasn't so sure Piper had what it took to try and save the lives from my visions…or to solve the mystery of their murders when Orwin and I were too late to prevent the victim's death. Piper didn't seem to have the moral or physical toughness this kind of work required. "Besides, I have a life here. Bedford is where I grew up. My family and friends are here, and I'm still learning the ways of my coven."

As hard as it was to admit, it was time to cut my losses.

Wise choice, Miss Lilura.

"Then you should stay here, Piper," I relented, clearly seeing that taking Piper with us on this hunt was no longer a viable option. Talk about a crushing realization. "I was hoping you could help us, and it's now obvious that your powers don't extend to hexes cast by the only known Lich queen in existence. I do appreciate you listening to my plea, though."

Piper parted her lips to reply, but Orwin's sudden presence in the chair next to her cut off her reply.

"I bought us a few minutes." Orwin pushed up his glasses as his gaze switched back and forth from Piper to me. "Well, can she help us or not?"

"No, she can't," I replied, forcing a smile to my lips.

I'd had a lot of setbacks in these last three months, and solving these murder mysteries for victims I couldn't save had taken its toll on my civil discourse. What I really needed now was to solve our current case quickly and then hit the road. Maybe I'd get lucky and not have another horrifically detailed vision for a couple of days. "Piper can't help us, and I need some quick answers."

"You mean she can't cure you, but she has decided to come with us, right?"

"No, she can't." I left it at that, and turned my focus on the murder. I cleared my throat in hopes that Orwin would follow my lead. With the druid blocking his powers, my partner couldn't hear my thoughts. Who knew I'd grown used to such a gross violation of my personal privacy? "Orwin, were you able to figure out who the druid is? I originally thought it could be Knox Emeric, but then I realized you read his thoughts at the gas station earlier. I think we can safely rule him out as our prime suspect. The faster we solve this mystery, the quicker we can be on our way out of this burg."

That would be best for everyone involved, Miss Lilura.

Orwin's eyes widened a bit when Pearl agreed with my sentiment. Granted, he hadn't had the time to experience hearing Piper's familiar constantly give her unsolicited advice during our conversation, but it wasn't like we'd have to deal with her anymore once we hit the road.

I did find it interesting that Pearl had no trouble

reading our thoughts and vice versa, but Orwin's gift had all but been shut down. That alone supported the druid angle pretty well. Orwin's self-protection ward only covered a spell aimed toward harming him personally, but what about Pearl?

A familiar's link to the supernatural is vastly different than the powers inherent to a gifted witch or warlock. Did you not take the history class of your coven, Miss Lilura?

"Just for the record, I know I'm right about Area 51," Orwin murmured, apparently deciding that now was the time to go head to head with a snooty familiar regarding conspiracy theories. "No need to go down that road with me again, unless you can offer me rock solid proof that the UFO crash never happen."

Is that your idea of a gauntlet, Mr. Cornelia?

"You'd be surprised at the vast amount of knowledge Pearl has managed to accumulate in her two thousand plus years." Piper stroked the sleek white fur as if Pearl were made of china. "She's a wealth of information, and comes from a very, very long line of special Egyptian familiars. In fact, her great grandmother belonged to Cleopatra, Queen of the Nile."

"Then why does she speak with an English accent?" I couldn't help but ask, regarding Pearl warily.

Speak to me directly, Miss Lilura. As for your inquiry, the financial backer of the excavation employed an archeologist by the name of Howard Carter to explore the tomb. Oh, how I loved my Howard, but it was the Lord Carnarvon's daughter who had the gift, you see. I had no choice but to accompany her back to England. I remember my dear Evelyn fondly, and I do miss her so.

Orwin shot me a glance that told me I just might have been too hasty in my decision to abandon our quest to bring Piper along with us. It was basically a two for one, but I'm sure even Orwin could recognize the potential problems with that kind of arrangement— Piper wasn't cut out for the kind of life we'd chosen for ourselves based on our situation, and Orwin was allergic to virtually anything with fur.

Granted, there was a good chance that Orwin's allergies could be dealt with…well, whatever Piper did to heal someone of his or her minor ailments. It might be something he could ask her to do before we hit the road together—along with grilling Pearl about Area 51 in hopes of proving that at least one of his conspiracy theories were viable—but what I'd been hoping for in the grand scheme of things just wasn't going to be in the cards.

As for Pearl, I had no doubt that the sleek white feline familiar had the wherewithal to handle her own self should the need ever arise. I, for one, certainly didn't want to end up on her bad side while we were stuck here dealing with this mess.

In case you didn't notice, you're already chained to that particular pole, my dear.

"Orwin, just tell me what we're dealing with," I practically pleaded, really wanting to take my wounded ego and leave this town as quickly as possible. I'd truly trusted in the suggestion that Piper had been the answer to all of our prayers. My error in judgement was a hard pill to swallow. "Who do you believe is the—"

"Back up the train," Orwin ordered, pushing up his glasses once again as he leaned forward to rest his forearms on the table with a perplexed expression. "Did you tell Piper that you're not the only witch or warlock who has been on the receiving end of Ammeline's wrath? If we don't stop her rampage, our kind will be exposed and eventually cease to exist. It will be back to the good old days of burning witches at the stake. I, for one, do *not* want to go out that way."

"Wait," Piper exclaimed in astonishment. "What am I missing? Are we in danger?"

My sweet Piper, this is not our concern. You have much to learn before you could even consider going on such a quest like this, and it is best we bring this conversation to a close. Miss Lilura, I suggest you muzzle your partner.

"No, no, no," I reassured Piper while shooting Orwin a frustrating glance. Who would have thought that Pearl and I would ever be on the same side? "You have nothing to worry about, Piper. Ammeline can't sneak up on me without notice. I made sure to cast a proximity spell so that I would be given a sense of her location should she be anywhere within a hundred miles of us."

"That doesn't mean another warlock or witch won't be sent along to do her bidding," Orwin muttered underneath his breath, glaring at Pearl as if this were all her fault. He seemed to have forgotten that he worked for me and that I paid him a hefty paycheck to follow my lead, clearly deciding that he would override my executive decision to abandon our plan of bringing Piper with us. Then again, he did have a personal stake in all of this. "Piper, we've been stuck traipsing around the country for the last three months attempting to save people from dying. Lou here receives a vision of the victim before he or she is murdered. Sometimes we make it there in time, and other times we arrive too late to do much of anything but catch the person responsible."

I won't say that you haven't been hexed but good, Miss Lilura, but it is still in everyone's best interest that the two of you be on your way. You need to do something about your warlock.

"Temp—I mean, Lou—told me what has been happening to the both of you, and I can't imagine having to deal with that on a daily basis."

"Let's just say that I'm not in any hurry to see another body. It's disconcerting, to say the least." My gaze landed on the young man who'd been on his computer during the time the woman's body was found. "Orwin, were you able to pick up anything from that young man before the druid stepped in and shut down your ability?"

"No," Orwin said somewhat distractedly. He wiped his nose with a napkin as he focused on Pearl. "You know something, don't you?"

"Pearl?" Piper asked, her sweet voice almost a magic of its own. There was such an innocence about her that it was really hard to lie to her. "If there is something you know that can help Lou and Orwin, please tell them now."

Pearl's green eyes narrowed as she contemplated Piper's request. As much as her familiar might give off such a superior air, it was clear that she loved her host very, very much. Piper was definitely her Achilles' heel.

It has been said that Ammeline's immortality could cause her to go insane in the nearly three hundred years she's been trapped here on this earth in her decaying body. Now, go forth in your quest. We wish you luck.

Chapter Five

"AS MUCH AS it pains me to admit this," Orwin muttered, sitting back in the chair as we both watched Piper go with the officer to give her statement, "that sarcastic white ball of Egyptian cotton could come in handy."

"It'll never work." I audibly sighed my utter frustration, having had incredibly high hopes that Piper would be the answer to my prayers. She wasn't even close to the answer I needed. "Piper is too much of a babe in the woods. She's far too trusting, and she'd only hinder us from solving the murder mysteries that fate has all but been forced to email straight to my head."

As I had previously mentioned, I hadn't had a premonition of anyone's murder in almost a week. It had taken us only four days to solve the aforementioned man's murder. I hadn't realized just how many days had passed since I'd envisioned Albert Wallace's death. He'd been bled dry by the time we found him, courtesy of a brood of vampires outside of Cincinnati, Ohio.

Nasty things, those bloodsuckers.

"I bet Pearl knows all kinds of things about how to neutralize vampires, werewolves, and goblins." Orwin sniffled as he tried to clear his sinuses. "I mean, besides the obvious…silver to bring down a werewolf, dragging vampires out into the sunlight before driving a pine garden stake from the local hardware store through their chest, and cold iron to kill a goblin. That vampire business got kind of messy, though."

"You can't even breathe while in the same room with Pearl. Besides, you said yourself that being around a familiar would send you straight to an insane asylum," I pointed out, reaching for my jacket. It was no longer hot in here, and it was best that Orwin and I be ready to take our leave at a moment's notice. Having a druid in the mix made this situation rather unpredictable and dangerous. "Apparently, fate had other ideas than us having access to another ally and a healer to boot."

"You believe in fate, but you don't believe in coincidences. You see the problem with that, right?"

Orwin's sigh of frustration was hard to miss. He pulled out his cell phone, setting an all-time record for him not having his nose glued to the display for the last hour. He was a tech junkie and always chasing electrons for one purpose or another. No doubt he was pulling up information on druids to make sure we had all the facts and a list of their weaknesses.

To catch you up to speed on our process, we'd been living out of hotels for the past three months. It wasn't like I'd been afforded a lot of privacy as of late, which was the reason I was currently debating on investing in one of those fully outfitted RVs. I'm not talking the small ones that wouldn't do me any good with Orwin's particular talent, but one that offered me the luxury of having a small bit of privacy and a base of operations.

Of course, it would have to be one of those luxury coach jobs that could pull my Jeep and provide us a functional headquarters to work out of while we were on the move. It would allow us to carry more supplies, a wide range of weapons, and a library of magic tomes for reference. As it stood, Orwin spent a great deal of time trying to track down arcane volumes of some sort or other. The footlocker we had for them was full to bursting in the back of the Jeep.

I guess it didn't matter now.

Without Piper joining us, an RV would be nothing more than an added expense for just the two of us. Although, mental health *was* important, right?

"I can't believe I'm saying this, but this silence might be the thing that sends me over the edge." Orwin never looked up from his phone, though he continued to provide me with information. "We can cross Knox Emeric off the list, as well as the three men who were with me in line."

"Really?" I casually glanced over to the table that was currently occupied by three suits who were all staring toward the restroom. My current position was somewhat blocked by the large condiment station. "Why is that?"

"I was close enough to all of them to pick up on some of their thoughts, and not one of them gave me the impression they were anything other than the average male wondering how many points they would score in this weekend's fantasy football league."

"Then that leaves the older couple, the two college girls, the young male who seems to be almost as techy as you, and the victim's three friends." I wasn't surprised when two men came around the corner with a gurney and began to cart out the body in a long zippered black bag. I was quick to try and fixate on everyone's expression, but all I could make out was shock, horror, and disbelief. "It is possible that someone snuck into the restroom, stabbed the victim, and then quickly left the café without anyone being the wiser."

Orwin had already pointed out that the café didn't have security cameras on the inside. This was a small town, and the crime rates were too low to justify the cost. I had a feeling that something of this nature might change their mind rather quickly.

"He or she would have had to walk past our table to leave the restrooms, and I would have definitely noticed someone internally freaking out if they had just stabbed someone. So, either he or she didn't walk past me or the culprit wasn't a newb. If the killer isn't working with a full deck, it's possible he or she could have kept his or her demeanor and not had a second thought about what he or she had done." Orwin finally put his phone down, his black boot bouncing continuously so that his knee went up and down incessantly. His nervous energy was beginning to show itself. "If we go on the assumption that no one in the café is that cruel and heartless, then that can only mean the victim was stabbed before we came in or that she'd been in there for a while."

"Which leaves the real possibility that the killer *did* leave before we entered the café and I stood in line for a coffee." I was coming to accept that the killer might not be inside this very room. It was clear that Orwin didn't share the same belief. "It's possible."

"No," Orwin denied, sliding his cell phone back into the pocket his jacket and leaning forward to give me his recollection from earlier. "We walked in. The older couple hadn't been at their table yet. I distinctly remembering the woman—"

"Marna."

"You know her name?" Orwin asked in surprise before waving his hand in dismissal. "You got that information from Pearl, didn't you?"

"Piper," I supplied, wondering just what else the petite blonde witch knew about our suspects. "We need to speak with her again before these witnesses are released. I'll try and stall the officer when it's my time to give a statement. Go on about the older couple. They're new around town, which means they still have some secrets."

"Marna was waiting at the pickup counter for their drinks, while…"

Orwin was waiting for me to supply him with the older gentleman's name.

"Jack."

"While Jack was over near the area where the café keeps their complimentary newspapers." Orwin narrowed his dark gaze at the couple who were now talking in hushed tones after the door had finally closed. There was still a forensics team in the restroom, and two officers were standing around eyeing the lemon loaf while the third took statements. It wasn't clear which officer had taken the lead, but that would be the individual I'd need to speak to in order to gain more insight into the murder. "I never had the opportunity to pick up on their mental thoughts with all the commotion earlier."

Orwin explained to me one time what it was like to have every single person's thoughts in his head who were gathered closely around him, and it wasn't pretty. It was basically a complete overload of information as everyone talked at once. I could see why he hadn't picked up on anything of importance, and it appeared now a druid had shut down Orwin's ability to use his power.

Have you thought of possibly thinking outside the box?

Orwin immediately stood and pushed back his chair as Pearl's advice practically came out of nowhere. I mean, sure, she was being held by Piper while answering the police officer's questions, but her posh tone had literally smashed the silence in our heads into tiny little pieces.

I didn't take either one of you for the dramatic types. Duly noted. Anyway, a druid can be downright cunning, and he or she has probably already thought of their exit strategy.

Knox Emeric was now staring at Orwin in curiosity, as was a few of the other witnesses. I reached out and tugged on his hand, hoping that everyone just thought he was antsy due to the situation we'd found ourselves in.

"Sit down," I whispered, deciding that it might be best to just get a list of names and investigate tomorrow. "You're drawing too much attention to us."

Orwin reluctantly sank back into his chair, though he never once took his skeptical gaze off Pearl. To anyone else, he was staring at Piper…and she was almost finished speaking to the officer, according to his body language.

Pay attention now, Miss Lilura. I want this evening over with as much as you do.

That much I could believe.

You just recited your suspect list, but you seem to be forgetting the other employees who were working this evening—another barista by the name of Tad Whitaker and the manager, whose name is Jamie Lehman.

"That's it?" Orwin whispered, clearly expecting Pearl to give us a bit more information. I was too, but she remained silent. "You're absolutely right, Lou. Bringing

Piper and Pearl along wouldn't be in our best interests, since they don't have anything to offer. Hey, it looks like you're next to give your statement."

Sure enough, Piper was holding Pearl a little closer to her chest as she made her way back to the table. Her blue eyes held a bit of confusion, which had me wondering if Pearl's statement regarding her colleagues hadn't jarred her memory.

"Orwin, see what Piper knows about Tad Whitaker and Jamie Lehman," I whispered, standing up when the police officer indicated that I was next up to give my statement. "And don't instigate anything with Pearl. I really don't want to have to take you to the ER for stitches or cat scratch fever."

Orwin's response to my censure was to cross his arms over his chest. All I could do was hope he came out of the next five minutes without a bleeding red exclamation mark down the middle of his face from the damage Pearl would no doubt leave behind in order to make her point.

I can make my point without drawing a single claw, Miss Lilura. You would do well to remember that.

Chapter Six

"…AND THAT IS when I rushed into the restroom behind the barista," I concluded, finishing up my statement. I was grateful I'd put on my jacket for the added warmth. "There was nothing we could do for her, though."

"We appreciate your cooperation," Officer Bell said as he closed the small cover on his writing pad. He was with the Bedford Police Department, and I was pretty sure he had some understanding of who and what might reside throughout his jurisdiction. "Will you be in town for a few days should Detective Jones have any more questions?"

Don't get me wrong about my previous observation.

Officer Bell hadn't come right out and said that he was aware a coven of witches was in the midst of his town. I'm pretty sure it came down to the way he'd worded his questions—like the one where he asked if I'd seen any unusual lights coming from the restroom before the victim was found. Who would inquire about such a thing unless they were aware banshees and grim reapers walked among us?

It did cross my mind that he could in fact be the druid, but why block the powers of others? Officer Bell hadn't been in the café during the time of the murder, anyway. If he was a druid working for the police and truly wanted to catch the guilty party, he would have used his abilities to his advantage. Same went for a warlock, which left me wondering if he wasn't a mere human trying to prove his own theory.

That alone made him almost as dangerous as a druid.

"My…cousin and I will be staying at the motel on the east side of town." I'd already given Officer Bell my cell phone number. It was easier to claim that Orwin and I were cousins than to explain our working relationship. "We can—"

The bell above the front entrance rang, causing every single witness and officer in the café to look that direction. It seemed that Detective Jones had finally arrived at the scene of his own investigation, and it was clear he'd already had one heck of a night.

Orwin's sudden sneeze from the table had caught Detective Jones' attention, but not for long. His dark gaze swept the witnesses gathered near the front of the café until his focus landed on Knox Emeric. It was clear the two men didn't like each other on sight, but I couldn't pinpoint the reason.

Testosterone, Miss Lilura. Apex predators give off pheromones.

Pearl was probably right. Alpha males would always

bump heads, but I'd learned over the last three months to never rule anything out. It didn't help that I could cut the tension with the proverbial knife. What was it about Knox Emeric that bugged me?

"Detective, I've taken everyone's statement and contact information," Officer Bell offered up, stepping away from me. I quietly made my way back to the table where Oliver, Piper, and Pearl were watching the newcomer closely. "The victim's name is…"

Officer Bell and Detective Jones began to make their way to the back of the café, giving me time to find out what new details Oliver was able to obtain from Piper. I quickly took my former seat, hoping that Piper or Pearl had provided Orwin with enough facts on those involved to solve this murder.

"Can we go now?" Orwin muttered, shooting me a look of irritation that I couldn't miss. Apparently, I'd been way off base with how vital Piper and Pearl could be in this situation. "It would be nice to be able to breathe sometime today."

You could always step outside, Mr. Cornelia. Don't let the door hit you in the—

"Pearl!" Piper exclaimed in embarrassment. Pearl didn't seem the least bit fazed, and she even hopped down from her witch's lap in order to start cleaning her paws as if she'd done nothing wrong. "I'm so sorry. Like I said before, Pearl can be a bit finicky, but it's only because she's so protective of me. She means well."

"Did she mean well when she brought up Roswell?" Orwin asked, pushing his glasses up the bridge of his nose to glare Pearl's way. His allergies evidently weren't the cause of his bad mood. It appeared that Pearl had figured out his weakness and was using it toward her advantage. "I happen to know for a fact that—"

"Orwin, we don't have time for your conspiracy theories," I responded gently, understanding all too well what would happen if we all let this conversation get out of hand.

"Pearl and I will help you figure out who killed Cassie Grier," Piper offered up with a small smile. She was attempting to appease everyone, but all that did was confirm her need to be a peacemaker. I had a gut feeling that she put herself in that spot a lot. "Orwin explained a bit of your process in solving these mysteries, Lou. I think it's fascinating the lengths you go to in order to save those you see in your visions or to at least see that the person responsible for his or her death gets what's coming to them."

Fix this problem that you've created, Miss Lilura. I can sense the change in her.

No wonder Pearl and Orwin were ready to attack one another. For some reason, Piper seemed to find our Scooby Doo method of investigating crimes rather interesting. Pearl had nothing to worry about, because I could dispel any notion that what we do was like what she's seen on the Saturday morning cartoons.

"Piper, did you know Cassie Grier?" I asked, having already decided that the barista's input in this murder investigation was pivotal. Once this mystery was solved, Orwin and I would be on our way…leaving Piper and Pearl in peace. "Is there anything you can tell us about the victim?"

"I didn't know Cassie personally." Piper rested an elbow on the table before gesturing with her eyes to the three women who'd come into the café with Cassie. "Vickie, Heather, and Megan were her closest friends. I think they might have all been friends from the community college, but I'm not one hundred percent sure about that. They all stopped into the café tonight after their yoga class."

I kept my opinion to myself regarding the so-called friendship between the four women. Cassie had definitely been the outsider, and that might have had something to do with her murder.

Poor Miss Cassie. She always did have the collywobbles.

Orwin slipped his fingers underneath his black-rimmed glasses and pinched the bridge of his nose in obvious frustration. He had more patience than I would have guessed in this situation. It was also quite refreshing to know he couldn't hear my opinion of him now that his abilities had somewhat been tabled.

"Collywobbles means that Cassie was always a bit nervous," Piper offered, frowning when Orwin audibly sighed and sat back in his chair. "Pearl is just trying to be helpful."

"Why was Cassie anxious?" I asked before Orwin disagreed with Piper's observation. "Was she a…"

Good heavens, no! Cassie was as human as you are hexed, Miss Lilura.

Well, when Pearl put it like that…

"Cassie was always a bit shy." Piper's eyes widened a bit, drawing our attention to the fact that Detective Jones and Officer Bell had come back from their little trip through the crime scene. "Honestly, I think that Vickie, Heather, and Megan felt sorry for Cassie."

A nest of vipers, those three.

I wouldn't have thought it possible, but this was the second time this evening that Pearl and I agreed on something.

"May I have your attention?" Detective Jones called out, his deep voice containing a rather raspy quality that gave away the fact that he was a heavy smoker. "I'd like to speak with Tempest Lilura, Orwin Cornelia, Daniel Wilson, Michael Harris, and Caleb Parker. The rest of you are free to go, but please know that I might be reaching out to some of you with follow-up questions."

Sighs of relief could be heard by those who had been released from the confines of the café. It didn't take a rocket scientist to figure out why Orwin, myself, and those three gentlemen who'd been in line were the individuals chosen to be re-questioned. After all, we had been the ones closest to the scene of the crime.

"Oh, and Jamie Lehman." Detective Jones was focused on the list of names that Officer Bell had given him. He was wearing what could only be called a trench coat that had seen better days. He reminded me of that old television show "Columbo". It might only need to be sent to the cleaners to have the wrinkles removed, but I'm not sure what good that would do when the man spent most of his waking hours traveling from crime scene to crime scene. His tenacity reminded me a lot of…well, me. Without the wrinkled clothes, of course. "Would it be possible to get us some fresh coffees?"

It didn't surprise me when Piper immediately jumped up to fulfill the man's request. She certainly was a people pleaser.

Which is why I'll be of assistance to you until this situation we've found ourselves in is over…and you can be on your way.

"I can get everyone some coffee," Piper said after her manager had given her approval. "I'll have it ready in a couple of minutes."

Pearl was now on the floor, gracefully strolling around Orwin's chair until she came to mine. The majestic way she sat back on her haunches left no doubt that she considered herself royalty.

You assume I'm not royalty, Miss Lilura. It seems to me as if you really need to brush up on your history. Crypt cats were considered companions of the Gods…that was until my move to England in the early twenties with my dear Evelyn.

"I just thought of something." Orwin had lowered

his voice to all but a mumble, making sure those passing our table in order to head for the door couldn't hear him. "Can you...you know."

Orwin flicked his wrist to indicate my ability to move things.

Your friend is wondering if the druid has smothered every supernatural creature's innate power in this close proximity or just his, thereby letting us know that the druid is completely aware of our presence.

Great. Pearl was translating now.

A simple thank you would suffice.

I inhaled and counted to ten. I'd said it before, but I completely understood why Orwin became irritated when my thoughts constantly invaded his personal space. Traveling in the Jeep hours on end, it was a wonder he hadn't gone insane.

Well, Miss Lilura, that might very well be the case considering he believes in little green men with antennas sticking out of their heads.

Orwin's cheeks became just as red as his nose.

"We don't have time for bickering," I reminded him, casting Pearl a look that told her she needed to rein in her impulses to instigate Orwin. Who was I kidding? She was doing it to me, too. "Go help Piper make the coffee or keep her company."

Orwin was onto something, and I couldn't afford to be distracted. It wasn't like we all had some internal transmitters that alerted each other when another supernatural being was in our vicinity. At least, not unless one specifically cast a precise incantation to do so, as I had with Ammeline.

There was only one way to find out if the druid was targeting only Orwin or anyone with supernatural powers. It would stand to reason that if the druid had murdered the victim that he or she would cover their bases, so I wasn't surprised to find that I couldn't even budge one of the empty plastic coffee cups on a random table.

"It seems as if no one with certain…ingrained abilities…can utilize their gifts."

Well, isn't that unfortunate? Do you resort to the human method of investigating often in situations like these?

"One of us needs to go outside with the others," Orwin said, already pushing his chair back and completely ignoring Pearl. What he really meant to say was that he needed to be the one to join the other witnesses, while at the same time get some distance from the vexing feline. "I'll be able to do my thing, and maybe then we'll be able to catch the killer."

The type of spell cast by the druid wouldn't have extended to the outdoors unless it was utilized on a specific person. If that were the case, we'd have to assume the area of effect was the café in general. Orwin would be able to rule out those individuals leaving as the guilty party, thus leaving the druid as our only suspect.

If this is the method the two of you use to close a case, it's a wonder any of them get solved.

"Lou." Orwin said my name in a manner that confirmed he was losing patience, when our roles were usually reversed. "Do something."

By this time, most everyone Detective Jones allowed to leave had already walked through the door. Knox Emeric was the last, and he was taking his good old time zipping up his backpack.

"Spill it," I warned Pearl, not in the mood for any games. "If you know something, then just tell us."

Did it ever occur to you that if the druid's magic can't touch a familiar that I must be able to tune in to his or her thoughts? What I'm trying to say, Miss Lilura, is that I know exactly who your druids are.

It didn't escape me that Pearl had used the plural sense in her declaration, leaving me to assume that the familiar could only be talking about Jack and Marna— the older couple who were new to town.

Now that we've established my value in this current predicament we've found ourselves in, let's get these interviews over with so that you and Mr. Cornelia may be on your way. Far, far away.

Chapter Seven

"THAT WAS A total waste of time and effort," Orwin complained, hoisting his overnight bag from the back of the Jeep. He was breathing a bit easier, just in case you were wondering. "Listen, Detective Jones seems to know what he's doing. We can just leave it to him and head out in the morning. He has all the information we do, with the exception of knowing about the druids."

I'd parked right in front of the two rooms we'd reserved side by side at the motel right outside of town. It certainly wasn't fancy, but we'd gotten used to places like these. It was basically one row of numerous rooms, each denoted by a tacky blue door with a dull gold number. No technological advancement here—a good old-fashioned key with the same blue color tag was our only way inside.

You should know that I never had any intentions of dipping into the trust fund that my parents had left me—it was their way of showing love—but these were dire times. My life was basically at stake, but I did have every intention of replacing every dime that was spent on this trek.

With that said, I had no idea how long it would take to get rid of this hex. It was best to conserve resources when and where we could, which basically extended to all things electronic for Orwin. Oh, and that RV that would no doubt give both of us a bit of sanity.

"We aren't leaving town until Cassie Grier's killer is behind bars."

I reached into the back of the Jeep and fished out my own overnight bag. We traveled light in terms of clothing, but we'd brought along Orwin's entire library of magic tomes and all of his computer equipment he swore he couldn't live without. We'd had to cast a spell on the vehicle to ensure that no one would be able to steal the items stored inside.

"I thought you'd say that," Orwin sighed in frustration as he closed the back end of the Jeep. "I'll look into Jack and Marna, see if we can confirm Pearl's assessment that they had nothing to do with Cassie's death."

Pearl's unexpected declaration had been somewhat of a shock. Now that particular familiar was full of useful information—not that I was acquainted with any other kinds of familiars. Maybe they were all a wealth of historical facts, and I should reconsider calling one forth myself.

"Don't even think about it," Orwin warned, walking around the Jeep and heading toward his room. "That clawed demon would be the death of me."

Orwin was probably right, but my agreement on leaving town with just the two of us had more to do with Piper's naiveté. She was just too pure for the gritty life that had all but landed in our laps.

"That, too," Orwin automatically agreed, as if we were having a conversation like normal people. "We're about as far from normal as we can get, Lou. Good-night."

I didn't have to tell Orwin to let me know immediately if he found any information to contradict Pearl's opinion of Jack and Marna. The white feline had been pretty adamant that the older couple had nothing to do with Cassie Grier's death, but I'd rather have confirmation of that before we completely ruled them out as suspects.

In just the four short hours that we'd been at the café—not that it had felt short at the time—I'd come to expect Pearl's English accented voice to buzz in my ear. Thankfully, it was blissfully quiet after eleven o'clock at night in the motel parking lot.

Well, sort of.

The faintest sound of muffled footsteps could be heard heading my way. I'd already taken inventory of my surroundings and had spotted a black Land Rover parked two slots down, and a beat-up old dark blue Chevy near the end. It stood to reason that the owner of the Land Rover had reserved a room near ours.

I'd wanted quarters for the vending machine, so I'd opened the driver's side door of my Jeep to reach into the console for some loose change. It was a good thing I had time to prepare for who was walking my way with a soda in one hand and a bag of chips in another.

It was none other than Knox Emeric.

From what I could see through the passenger side window, the man didn't seem to notice me. I somehow didn't believe that for a moment, and I tensed in preparation for some type of confrontation.

We'd run into each other three times in one day.

No one was that unlucky, right?

You already knew my thoughts on coincidences, so I very carefully backed my way out of the Jeep and waited for him to say or do something that warranted me to use witchcraft in the middle of a practically abandoned parking lot. I'd have to chance exposing myself if it came down to self-defense.

Without a glance or a word, Knox Emeric quietly let himself into a room two doors down from mine.

"Wasn't he at the café?"

I barely caught the scream that was about to fall from my lips, spinning around in irritation at the sound of Piper's voice.

"Don't do that!" I exclaimed through clenched teeth, resting a hand against my chest. My touch did nothing to calm my racing heart, but I'd instinctively curled my fingers into the palm of my hand so that I didn't mistakenly fling the poor girl into the side of the building. "Piper, what on earth are you doing here?"

I asked her that myself, Miss Lilura. What can I say? My charge is a stubborn one.

Sure enough, Pearl was sitting on the sidewalk no more than six feet away from Piper. The white familiar's tail seemed to have its own rhythm as it swayed from side to side. Every now and then, I could see the twitch of irritation, but she could just join the club.

No, thank you. I don't believe in exclusive clubs.

"I saw your father waiting for you outside of the café," I said to Piper, taking note that she must have parked down by the office of the motel. I closed the driver's side door to the Jeep now that any hint of danger in the form of Knox Emeric had evaporated. I was going to have to do a bit of research on the man myself if I were to have peace of mind about his sporadic presence. "I'm surprised your dad didn't take you home."

As I've already stated, my sweet Piper has a bit of a stubborn streak.

She also had Pearl, which was probably the only reason Piper's father could rest a bit easier.

"I *am* twenty-two," Piper reminded me as if I hadn't known that bit of information or the fact that Pearl had all but thrown her under the bus. Given Orwin's research, I pretty much knew everything about the young woman, including that she wasn't cut out for solving murder mysteries. Her father had been right to worry about her out in this dark, dark world. "I'd also like to point out that I'm no longer a girl. Anyway, I overheard you say to Detective Jones that you were staying at this motel, and I wanted to offer my help to cure Orwin of his allergies."

Piper had on one of those lightweight peacock coats in a bright pink color that matched her lip gloss. The brilliance of her ensemble, as well as her personality, were glaringly different from mine.

I'd like to keep it that way, if you please.

"I got it, Pearl," I replied irritably, hoisting my overnight bag over my shoulder and heading toward my room. It didn't take me long to fish out the motel key from my pocket in exchange for the quarters in the palm of my hand. "Orwin is next door, Piper. I'm sure that he'll appreciate your gesture."

It didn't take me long to slip the key into the lock and twist the door handle. The faintest scent of disinfectant hit me in the face, reminding me why investing in a high-end RV might be the wisest of choices. These out of the way motels that Orwin and I chose to stay in just weren't cutting it anymore.

I can see why. People have to be off their trolley to stay in a place like this. Is that...

A quick glance over my shoulder showed me that Pearl had taken a tentative step over the threshold, her green eyes glued to a stain in the carpet. I got the feline's drift, though. The crusty stain did look like blood, but my guess was that it was some type of wine or juice that had soaked into the well-worn carpet.

One could only hope.

"I was also hoping to speak with you." Piper followed Pearl's path, joining us inside the room until she was able to close the door behind her. She twisted her purse strap around her hand as she thought over whatever it was that she'd rehearsed on the way over here. "Jack and Marna are good people, regardless of the fact that they're druids. They live a quiet life, and they'd like to be left alone in peace."

My sweet Piper has a point. Where most druids allow the capability of great power to go to their heads, this older couple would like to blend into society to live out the rest of their days in peace.

I let my overnight bag slide from my shoulder onto the bed, utter exhaustion flowing through me. All I wanted was a good night's sleep. Tomorrow was another day, and Orwin and I had already mapped out our plans to speak with each suspect individually—and that included Jack and Marna.

I see that my dear Piper isn't the only one with a stubborn streak.

"Orwin and I have a system that hasn't failed us yet," I explained, debating on whether or not to leave my black leather jacket on to walk down to the vending machine. I suppose I could just drink the tap water and then fall into bed. Sleep was beginning to sound a lot better than food, anyway. Having someone in my head nonstop was mentally exhausting. No wonder Orwin could nap anywhere and at any time. "Piper, I truly appreciate you coming here to help Orwin. It was a sweet gesture that I'm sure he'll appreciate somewhere down the line. As for Cassie Grier's murder, it's probably best that you stay clear of us while we do our investigating. I might not have seen the woman's murder, but I can't in good conscience leave here with her killer still walking the streets. The perp is dangerous, and I don't want him coming after you."

You might not be so bad, Miss Lilura. As I suggested earlier, come back to us in fifty years or so to see if we can't do something about that hex of yours. Wait. We adjusted that timeline to sixty years, didn't we?

Sixty years? With all the time and effort Orwin and I were putting into finding Ammeline, it had better not take me sixty years to lift this hex. Besides, the rate at which the Lich's mental capacity was being eroded over time…I wasn't so sure our kind had sixty years.

For once, it seemed as if Pearl didn't have two cents to share with me on that last observation.

I'm mulling it over, Miss Lilura. Don't rush me.

"I'm sure Orwin is still awake if you…"

I let my words trail off as Piper and Pearl became somewhat blurry, and it was all I could do to remain standing.

No, no, no.

This couldn't be happening, especially with Cassie Grier's killer still out there.

I fought against my curse with every ounce of

strength I had, but my attempt was futile, as always. There was nothing I could do to stop the garish vision from unfolding in front of me as it replaced everything within sight.

Piper was calling my name, but I couldn't respond.

I was suddenly in the parking lot of a mall, watching from afar as Jamie Lehman laid on the cold, wet cement with a hand over her side. Her breathing was shallow as she tried to call for help. No one could hear her as her life began to seep away with each second that ticked by on her watch.

Just as suddenly as I was taken to the future, I was dragged back to the present.

"…you okay? Was it one of your visions?" Piper continued to bombard me with questions, but she'd never witnessed the aftereffects of my hex. It wasn't pretty, and I didn't turn down her offer to help sit on the edge of the bed. "Did you really see someone just die? Let me go get Orwin from next door."

I remained silent as Piper quickly left the room, even closing my eyes to stop the room from spinning. It always took me a moment to collect my composure.

That was bloody awful!

I'd completely forgotten that Pearl was still in the room. I finally lifted my lashes now that the walls and ceiling had stopped spinning. The usually composed, sleek white familiar had a few hairs out of place. Truthfully, it appeared as if she'd been put through the wringer.

I blinked a few times, thinking maybe my vision hadn't returned to normal.

No, Pearl was still looking somewhat disheveled.

"Pearl?" I was hesitant to ask, and I even put my hand on the bed to steady myself. My heartrate once more began to beat faster at the realization that I might not be as alone in this mess as I'd thought. "Did you just see…?"

Pearl shook herself like a wet dog, not that she'd appreciate the analogy. She even had to catch herself from wobbling by suddenly plopping down on her haunches with an ungraceful splat.

Well, isn't that just a fly in the ointment?

Chapter Eight

MY GROAN OF agony was instantaneous as a streak of pain tore through my shoulder blade when I tried to lift my head.

Ouch!

"…don't think you know anything about Area 51," Orwin complained, his voice a little too loud in an enclosed vehicle. His sneeze told me immediately that Pearl was inside the car. "I've done my research. Trust me, the government is holding back vital information from the public. Piper, do you have a box of tissues in here?"

I lifted my arm and rested my hand against the crick in my neck as I pried my eyes open. It was as if I had a hangover from drinking a fifth of tequila. The first thing I was able to focus on was that I'd somehow ended up in the backseat of Piper's Prius instead of the front seat.

Trust me, it hadn't been much of a shock to find out that the petite blonde drove a hybrid.

Anyway, Orwin and I had gotten into the habit of collecting blankets and snacks for times like these, but

Piper's Prius wasn't equipped with the usual stakeout essentials. With all the books and computer equipment in the Jeep, there would have been no way to bring Piper and Pearl along even if we'd wanted.

Don't get me wrong, I had done my best to convince them that they should go home, but they'd insisted on seeing this case through to the end.

I'd also somehow ended up with Pearl as my backseat companion.

Did you know that you snore, Miss Lilura? Sleep apnea is a real health hazard. You should have that looked into soon.

I was directly behind the driver's seat, so it was easy for me to reach out and smack Orwin upside the head when he'd unconsciously nodded in agreement. His exclamation of surprise had turned into another sneeze.

"If you'd reverse the spell you put on yourself to protect you against Ammeline, then I'd be able to rid you of those allergies," Piper tried to reason, clearly having gotten nowhere with that argument. Those two had bickered half the night while we kept watch over Jamie Lehman. This was one of the few occasions that I'd been given time to save a victim from one of my prophesies, and I wasn't going to let the woman go about her life without having adequate surveillance. "What could happen in the few short moments it takes for me to—"

"Ask Lou," Orwin exclaimed, inadvertently glancing in the rearview mirror. He was still rubbing the back of his head. "Good morning, your highness."

I didn't realize that you were speaking to me.

"Don't you have to go for a walk or something? You know, like use the neighbor's flowerbed for something or other?" Orwin complained before wiping his nose with a tissue that Piper had produced from the glove compartment. The interior of her vehicle was a lot cleaner than the Jeep, and it also had enough room for three people…and apparently a cat. "I need air. And just to clarify, the spell I used to protect myself from the likes of Ammeline was rather involved and tedious. I'm not sure I'd be able to pull it off again without enough rest and study, so there's not a chance in this magical realm that I'd ever lift the protection enchantment for allergies that could be simply remedied by the removal of a certain familiar."

Does Mr. Cornelia always complain like this? He should be glad that he's alive and breathing at all, if you ask me.

Orwin cracked the window, but not before rolling his eyes for me to take notice of his frustration. It wasn't an easy process to get used to having other people in our cramped space, but both Piper and Pearl had made it impossible to leave the motel without them.

The custom motor coach made by Powerhouse Coach was looking better and better by the minute, even if Piper and Pearl weren't going to be joining our little detective team. They had available for sale a 2008 fifty-two-foot coach with four slide-outs, measuring just over four hundred square feet for a well-provisioned head-quarters. It also featured a Skydeck, which provided another two hundred and seventy-one square foot area as an elevated observation deck for stakeouts and defensive positions.

We'd be living in the lap of luxury rather than being exposed to those nasty germs at those cheap hotel rooms we'd been spending so much time in lately. That mobile queen-sized bed was sounding pretty good right about now.

"How are you feeling, Lou?" Piper asked, her concern still evident. I'd scared her last night, but not as much as I'd freaked out Pearl. It turned out that because familiars could hear the thoughts of witches and warlocks, she'd had a direct link to the hex that had been placed upon me. "It took Pearl a while to catch her breath, too."

All things come to those who wait, my sweet Piper. That spot of warm cream did me right up.

My visions were physically, mentally, and emotionally draining. I could see why it would have taken Pearl some time to get use to the aftermath. It was why I couldn't keep my eyes open past two o'clock in the morning, which meant that Orwin had been keeping watch for at least four hours nonstop.

Maybe next time you'll take my advice on the warm cream, Miss Lilura.

"Could we please stop with the surname business?" I

groaned, going against my better judgement. "Lou is fine, Pearl."

The white feline curled one side of her mouth, allowing her perfectly aligned whiskers to lift in disdain.

I was taught to mind my manners, Miss Lilura. Turn of the century England had certain standards of behavior, you know. Lords and ladies were cultured back then.

I sighed in resignation before putting my hand against the vent below the console. The heat was most welcoming. Orwin had the engine running, which meant it had gotten quite cold in the middle of the night. We were currently parked on the other side of the street from Jamie Lehman's house, but three people in a Prius were bound to draw attention from those about to leave for work. We'd have to make an operational plan very soon.

Please explain to me why we are here if Ms. Lehman was attacked at the mall. Your methods are somewhat confusing.

I struggled to sit up a little straighter, finally stretching my arms and neck so that I didn't do any more damage than I already had by falling asleep against the window. I shouldn't have allowed either Piper or Pearl to tag along, but I hadn't wanted to waste time arguing when another woman's life was on the line.

As I said earlier, we'll help you and Mr. Cornelia due to Piper's involvement at the café. Once this situation has resolved itself, you'll leave town and won't come back for a minimum of sixty years as we've agreed upon.

"We're not letting Jamie Lehman out of our sight," I

finally said, my voice a bit hoarse with sleep. I cleared my throat and tried again while carefully surveying our surroundings, immediately noticing that Jamie's next-door neighbor had turned on a light in their living room. As for Pearl's commentary, it was pointless to argue with her when we were both in agreement. Having them along full-time definitely wasn't an option. "The visions I have are usually accurate, but sometimes a few of the clues get mixed up. Orwin and I usually tag team on who watches the victim—if we get to him or her in time—and who looks into the possible motives for murder."

I'll admit that it sounds as if your methods are solid, but when does that leave you time to search for Ammeline?

Unfortunately, it didn't leave us with tons of free time.

Ahhh, that Lich is a smart one, isn't she?

"But we already know that Jamie's connected to Cassie Grier's murder," Piper pointed out, turning in the passenger seat so that she could get a better look at me while we talked. She'd put her hair into a pony tail, somehow making her look even younger. "It stands to reason we should go back to those suspects at the café. Since Orwin is the one with the gift of telepathy, it also stands to reason that I should accompany him to have a talk with those patrons who were at the café last night. My presence will make it easier to encroach on their personal space without having the suspects become too suspicious."

I didn't miss the way Orwin's eyebrow rose in admiration at Piper's suggestion of how we should work this particular case. Honestly, it was exactly what I would have suggested had those druids not been involved.

Agreed.

"What are you agreeing to, Pearl?" Piper asked, frowning as she searched my face for whatever it was Pearl and I had settled on.

We wouldn't want anyone to notice anything amiss, and your shift at the café starts at four o'clock this afternoon.

Pearl had definitely stretched the truth, which didn't tell me anything I didn't already know—she would go to any lengths to protect her charge.

As for the café opening their doors this morning, I'm sure the place would be crowded with people hoping to find out something about Cassie Grier's murder. I wouldn't want to be anywhere near that place today, but Orwin and I knew better than most that the killer sometimes returned to the scene of the crime.

Are you suggesting that I would lie to my sweet Piper, Miss Lilura? I would do no such thing, and I'm rather offended by your implication.

"I didn't say you would lie, Pearl, just that you might stretch the truth." I ran a hand over my face, wishing we'd thought to bring those thermoses we had in the Jeep. The amount of coffee they could hold was unbelievable, and I could certainly use a hit of caffeine. Of course, the RV would supply me with round the clock coffee. "Piper, I was just thinking to myself that your family wouldn't appreciate me drawing you into a murder investigation, and Pearl agreed. It's best if the two of you go about your normal day and allow Orwin and I to catch Cassie's killer."

I suppose I could join you after seeing that Piper is settled in at the café this afternoon.

I understood Pearl's offer, because familiars had the ability to appear and disappear at will. She'd be able to sneak into places we couldn't, supplying us with pertinent information vital to the case.

"You weren't worried about my family when you first tried to talk me into joining you and Orwin," Piper pointed out, fishing out another tissue without being prompted to when Orwin sneezed. "I'm not saying that Pearl and I would ever leave our home, but we can be of help to you while you're in town. Let me go with Orwin."

I can agree with that compromise if you can, Miss Lilura, provided that Piper stays within sight of Mr. Cornelia.

"We might need to take them up on their offer, Lou." The slight edge to Orwin's tone told me that he'd noticed something amiss. "Jamie's bedroom light just came on, which tells me that she's going somewhere. Piper already told me that Jamie doesn't work today. We're most likely running out of time."

Oh, dear!

Orwin was basing his assumption of time on the fact that the murders usually happened within twenty-four hours from the time I had a vision. An attempt on

Jamie's life would be most likely happen sometime today.

Then we have not a single minute to spare. There's the door, Miss Lilura. Go on, now. We have places to be and people to see.

"I hate to break this to you, Pearl, but it is you who has to get out of the vehicle."

Oh, no, no, no, Miss Lilura. You have that wrong.

I'd run through our options, and there was only one way we could catch the murderer in the timespan provided.

There are any number of ways this can be done, oh mighty hexed one.

I inhaled deeply and counted to ten, reminding myself that it was best I not be dragged into a spitting match before I'd had my coffee.

"Pearl, you're going to go inside Jamie's residence and keep an eye on her. The moment she decides to leave the house, you come to me—not Orwin and not Piper, but me," I clarified, wanting to make sure that Pearl understood the importance of the duties assigned to her. I'm sure she would agree with me that we needed to keep Piper's involvement down to a minimum. "In the meantime, Orwin and Piper will drive me back to the motel so that I can pick up my Jeep. The two of you will go speak to the list of suspects while I go and have a talk with Jack and Marna. No one can tell me that two druids didn't notice something amiss last night. My bet? Those two know exactly who the killer is."

I want it on record that I do not agree with this most recent turn of events.

"Duly noted," I reassured her, waving my hand in the direction of Jamie Lehman's residence. "But this is the best chance we have at solving this mystery, thus allowing Orwin and I to be on our way."

Fair enough, Miss Lilura. Before I go, I'd like to clarify something with Mr. Cornelia.

"Oh, joy," Orwin exclaimed, still monitoring Jamie Lehman's house for anything amiss. "I promise that I won't let anything happen to Piper while we're gallivanting around town interviewing the witnesses."

I'm sure that Pearl had a lot of rules and regulations for Orwin now that he had Piper in tow for the remainder of the day. Surprisingly enough, the white feline had a dry sense of humor.

I just thought I should warn a conspiracy theorist such as yourself that the town of Kecksburg is but an hour from here—where the supposed unidentified flying object crash landed in 1965. If I were you, I'd be on the lookout for little green men, Mr. Cornelia. They can be sneaky little buggers.

Chapter Nine

"PEARL WAS JUST having a bit of fun," Piper said in defense of the antagonizing familiar, even smiling to try and lessen the sting of being baited by a cat. "You should be honored that she feels I'm safe enough to leave me with you for the day."

Orwin remained silent, probably stewing over the fact that the town of Kecksburg was only an hour away. I'm sure it had crossed his mind, but Pearl just had to pull the conspiracy lever. With my luck, he'd want to check out the so-called UFO crash site after this case was over.

"You know I can hear you, right?" Orwin asked, lifting that straight and narrow black eyebrow above his glasses on the right side as he made eye contact with me in the rearview mirror. I was still in the backseat, but we were less than three minutes from the motel. "It's been three months."

I shrugged, letting him know that sometimes my mind was running a million miles a minute. All of my thoughts were focused on Jamie Lehman, plus it was kind of a relief not to hear that English accented running commentary.

As for Jamie, the only reason an attempt on her life would be made was if she'd seen something last night…or at least the murderer thought the café manager had witnessed something that could put the culprit away for life.

"Maybe Pearl and I should have stayed back and had a talk with Ms. Lehman." Orwin flicked on the turn signal of the Prius as he came to a stop sign on the edge of town. The colorful leaves were slowly falling from the tree branches onto the wet grass below. Pretty soon, the ground would be covered with snow and there would be no leaves to be found. "We can always head back that way after we drop you off at the motel."

"I plan to head back to Jamie's residence right after I'm finished speaking with Jack and Marna." The motel was now in sight, and so was the Land Rover that belonged to one Knox Emeric—not that I had been searching for his vehicle. Quite the contrary. I wanted to make sure that it was gone. Why *was* Knox Emeric in town? "Take Piper and go speak with Cassie's friends first. We know from experience that the murderer is usually someone the victim had a personal relationship with, and trust me when I say that they weren't the kind of friends I'd want in my life."

"Don't worry about that guy," Orwin advised, having picked up on the fact that I was worried about the stranger being in so many places we'd been over the last two days. "I was in his head, and all he thought about were gas prices and a good lightly grilled, peppercorn steak."

I was reminded once again that Orwin's gift was a blessing, and I didn't doubt that we'd have Cassie Grier's murderer delivered to Detective Jones by this evening.

"Keep in touch. If anything sticks out, let me know immediately." I opened the back door to Piper's Prius and climbed out, making sure I grabbed her attention. "Please listen to everything Orwin says today. Anyone who can kill in the manner that we saw last night won't hesitate to do so again without much more of a motive."

"Promise," Piper replied with another one of her smiles. I found it a little too bright under the circumstances, but it was clear that she was just excited to be a part of something so important. I couldn't blame her, but it was one of the reasons we'd made the wise decision to abandon the plan of bringing her along. "And don't worry. I'll try to convince him to let me take away his allergy issues."

I closed the back door of the Prius, instantly catching Orwin's pained expression. He didn't have to say a word. Under no circumstances was Piper ever going to talk him into doing something so foolish as letting down his guard.

As we'd mentioned before, it had taken Orwin close to two months to collect all the ingredients and to perfect his intricate spell of warding. To do so again would mean he'd be exposed for at least that long if not longer, especially considering that some of the spell components could only be found on the west coast under the light of a full moon.

Orwin eventually pulled away while Piper pointed in which direction he should take as they finally exited the parking lot on their quest for answers.

"You were at the café last night."

The Land Rover that was parked a couple slots from mine had done a good job of shadowing Knox Emeric. He must have been on the other side, though I don't know why he'd waited so long to show himself. The statement he'd made confirmed that he knew exactly who I was, but that wasn't what gave me pause.

"You're from Washington."

The license plate on the back of the Land Rover clearly displayed where the man was from, but I foolishly hadn't taken the time to look. I knew better than to ignore the obvious.

"I am," Knox agreed, transferring his keys to his left hand as he walked closer to me. He was wearing a pair of faded jeans with one of those thick plaid jackets that hadn't been in style for quite some time, yet he pulled it off as if he were the face of a rodeo ad. "My name is Knox Emeric. I was on my way to New York when I decided to stop in town and search for a place that had free Wi-Fi. Considering what happened there, I guess I should have kept driving."

It wouldn't have been very friendly of me to blurt out that I didn't believe in coincidences, so I did the only thing I could—I stuck out my hand when he'd offered his and held my breath when the warmth of his grip enveloped mine.

He was hot.

Wait.

That didn't come out the way I'd meant for it to.

Let me paraphrase—his body temperature was unusually hot. I couldn't make hide nor hair of the fact that Orwin hadn't picked up anything unusual from the man standing in front of me, but I was now convinced that something was definitely off with Knox Emeric— regardless of his thoughts.

I hadn't realized that his eyes were a light brown. In truth, they were practically gold, with just a hint of iridescence. His short black hair held a bit of dampness on the ends, revealing that he'd just recently had a shower. He hadn't bothered to shave off his five o'clock shadow, which told me either he liked it or he was just too lazy this morning to bother.

"It's nice to meet you," I replied with a forced smile, fully prepared to throw him thirty feet or more should he make any type of threatening move. "My name is Lou. It's a terrible thing that happened yesterday. I hope the police catch whoever could do something so horrible."

"I'm on my way to speak with Detective Jones right

now." Knox looked over his shoulder to where Piper's Prius was no longer in sight. "Is that where your friends are going?"

Going from a psychology professor to what was basically a private investigator hadn't been easy, but I had picked up a few things in the last three months. Knox was fishing for answers, similar to how I did when talking with suspects.

Was that it?

Did Knox Emeric actually believe that I murdered Cassie Grier?

"Actually, no," I replied to his inquiry on Orwin and Piper's destination. I forced the tension out of my shoulders. It wouldn't do to have him realize that I was on to whatever game he was playing, but I could definitely roll the dice. "I'm just here visiting friends, and one of them has to work today. It sounds as if you hadn't planned on spending the night in Bedford. I hope that you clear things up with Detective Jones, especially seeing as you were in the restroom prior to that poor woman being found."

In my defense of how rude I'd just come across, I'd been trying to figure out if he'd seen or heard anything unusual while using the café's restroom. I trusted Orwin when he said that Knox wasn't guilty of murdering Cassie Grier, but at the same time I recognized that Knox Emeric was hiding something.

Unfortunately, I didn't have Orwin here to help me

figure out all the pieces of the puzzle.

"I'm sorry," I apologized quickly, not wanting to make another enemy. I currently had my fill of those, including the queen bee of them all—Ammeline Letty Romilda. "That came out wrong. I was just implying that you could be of help to Detective Jones had you noticed anything unusual while you were in the back hallway."

"I understand," Knox assured me with a crooked smile that would have been rather charming had I not been so suspicious of his motives. "I wish I had seen something that could aid Detective Jones in his investigation, but all I remember is tripping over a white cat and then bumping into you. Well, I don't want to be late to my meeting with Detective Jones. Enjoy your day, Lou."

Knox gave me a slight nod before turning on his brown boots that reminded me of the military. I'd had a few students in ROTC who liked to wear them, which explained the underlying air of authority he displayed when walking. He was a very confident man, and also one to keep a close watch on while I was here in town. Men like him rarely missed anything, always taking in their surroundings for security reasons. It was an occupational hazard, and he had to have seen something that would lead Detective Jones to Cassie Grier's killer.

The Land Rover eventually followed the path of Piper's Prius, leaving me to stand alone in the parking lot of the motel. The urge to follow Knox was overwhelming, but it was best I stick to the plan we'd laid out this morning. If someone with former military experience hadn't noticed anything amiss last night, a druid certainly would…and there had been two.

Unfortunately, I had no doubt that the residence of druids would be completely enchanted with magic wards and runes. My own powers would be useless, but I had a little trick up my sleeve that Jack and Marna would never see coming.

Chapter Ten

THE ADDRESS PIPER had given me for Jack and Marna was in one of the quaint neighborhoods on the edge of town, completely opposite of what I would have expected. Typically, druids remained within their own groups spread across the world. They weren't much for neighborhood associations. For those who decided to break from their own kind, they usually preferred to be off the grid at the end of some far-off trailhead.

I'd parked in front of a typical two-story brick home that was very much like the others on the street. The front yard was immaculate, complete with a perfect pile of leaves that looked as if they'd just been raked. There was barely a leaf left on the large oak tree, and some of the bushes had already been covered against the bite of the coming frost with the upcoming winter.

The reason I hadn't gotten out of the Jeep was due to the fact that Jack was coming out of the house, closing the screened door behind him as he called out goodbye to his wife. I had to wonder if he hadn't received a call from Detective Jones, but I quickly dismissed that idea.

Marna would have no doubt accompanied her husband to the police station had they received such a request.

Jack even waved to the neighbor who'd walked outside in his robe to retrieve the morning's paper. The older gentleman signaled with his hand in recognition, but he didn't bother to look up from reading the latest headline—which no doubt covered the story of Cassie Grier's murder.

The next-door neighbor clearly wasn't a morning person like Jack, who was currently getting into his car. He'd been wearing one of those newsboy hats, but he'd taken it off before buckling up like a good upstanding citizen. It was clear that he was trying to fit in with the non-magical mundane neighbors.

They seem like genuinely nice people, do they not?

After everything I'd been through these last three months, I wasn't the type of woman to scream at a spider or squeal at the sight of blood. Dealing with vampires, werewolves, and such had me pretty used to the unexpected.

With that said, I'd never imagined having a familiar suddenly appear in the passenger seat of my vehicle without any prior notice. It was a wonder the top of my head hadn't hit the soft top of my Jeep when I literally startled enough to come out of my seat.

"Pearl!" I yelled, gripping the steering wheel as a means to calm my racing heart. Trust me, it didn't help in the least. "You can't do that kind of stuff! What were you thinking? You're lucky I didn't fling you through the side window."

That begs to question, my dear hexed one.

I leaned my head back on the headrest and closed my eyes, willing the adrenaline to leave my body before causing my twenty-eight-year-old self to have a heart attack. Evening out my breathing didn't seem to be helping, because my next inhalation caught in my throat when I realized the implications of her unexpected visit.

"Shoot," I muttered, quickly leaning forward and fumbling with the keys I'd already put in my jacket. "Where is Jamie? Is she driving to the mall? What time does the mall open, anyway? Why would she be—"

Aren't you all just doom and gloom, Miss Lilura? Ammeline really has done a number on you. You'll be happy to know that Ms. Lehman is just fine, thank you. She's currently in the police station waiting to meet with Detective Jones to go over yesterday's events.

"Then why are you here?" I whispered, casting a quick glance around the homes in our vicinity to make sure that no one was watching us. Having a dog inside a vehicle was one thing, but a cat? These townsfolk might think that having a cat inside my Jeep might be just a wee bit out of place. "I told you that you needed to stay with Jamie Lehman."

Are you questioning my work ethic? I will have you know that I take my assignments very seriously. Ms. Lehman is perfectly safe in a police station surrounded by law enforcement. She's currently waiting her turn while a Mr.

Knox Emeric goes back over his statement.

I'm not sure why it was a relief to know that Knox hadn't lied to me about where he was going today. It shouldn't have mattered either way.

Oh, no, no, no. Tsk, tsk. Trust me when I tell you that Mr. Knox Emeric is not your type.

"Not my type?" I reiterated in surprise, not sure where Pearl got that I'd be interested in the man at all based on my desire to want the truth. Just because he was handsome and I might have glanced at the way those jeans had practically molded themselves to his body did not mean I was interested in the man. "One, you don't know what my preferred type of man is, Pearl. Two, you need to learn that certain thoughts are private and not to be shared out of turn."

I didn't realize there was someone else in the vehicle that I could share such a shocking revelation with. Oh, wait. There isn't. While I'm pointing out the obvious, I'd also like to call attention to the fact that you might protest a little too much on the current subject matter. Just food for thought. Anyway, enough of this chitchat. I thought it best you have backup for when confronting these druids. In my past experience, they can be a bit tricky to deal with at times.

"I thought you said they were nice."

You're confusing me with Piper. I distinctly recall saying the older couple had nothing to do with Cassie Grier's murder, and I stand by my assessment. With that said, druids can be rather unpredictable and dangerous. Isn't that why you have enchanted powder in your pocket to prevent

Jack and Marna from drawing power from the limited amount of nature surrounding their home?

It was no use in chastising Pearl for once again spilling secrets aloud. Yes, I did have a creative weapon at my disposal when dealing with druids. In all honesty, Orwin and I had spent a lot of time creating enchanted items, such as the dust from the most northern lodestone of the Lough Gur Stone Circle in Ireland. It could prevent a druid from drawing on Mother Nature's power without them knowing the key phrases to properly align their magics to a powerful sigil.

The downside was that once the powder was discovered, the druids could use it to gain a fantastic amount of power very quickly. It had very little upside in the long run, but it was most effective in the short-term.

Weapon? Enchanted items? The Lough Gur Stone Circle? I wasn't aware we'd gone to war.

"Fine," I relented, watching Jack's car pull out of his driveway and head toward town. "Orwin and I have a magical arsenal at our disposal under the floorboard in the back of the Jeep. We take the occasional day out of a given week to add to our collection or boost our capabilities. Don't give me that look, Pearl. You've got no reason to lift your whiskers in disdain. Don't judge. There are some creatures that take a little more edge to defeat than our powers may be capable of handling in any given moment."

I never said a word in judgement, my dear hexed one.

"You're making me nervous by being here when you

should be with Jamie." I didn't want to waste any time now that Jack had left the house. Dealing with druids was hard enough, but two together? No, thank you. "Go back to the police station, and touch base with me later."

Ms. Lehman is just fine at the station while she waits her turn to speak with Detective Jones. You, on the other hand, are entering the unknown. It is not wise to do so alone.

"Why, Miss Pearl, are you worried about me?" I asked in mock disbelief. I wasn't able to stop myself from making fun of the familiar just a bit. Orwin and I might take our cases seriously, and the powers that be certainly understood my despair over my current situation, but we weren't as uptight as the prim and proper Pearl. "Fine. We'll go inside, ask our questions, and then leave…where you can then go and make sure that no one tries to kill Jamie Lehman while the rest of us continue to investigate."

Uptight? I will have you know that I—

I quickly opened the door to the Jeep and stepped out, having noticed the neighbor holding his paper staring at me just inside his front door. He'd been watching me ever since Jack had pulled out of the driveway, and it was best I not give the older man any suspicious ideas about why I was sitting in my vehicle while watching the houses in the neighborhood.

That was simply rude.

Hearing Pearl while not being able to see her was downright eerie, but I couldn't stop my advance toward

Jack and Marna's house. It was instinctive to verbally speak when in a conversation, but the neighbor would definitely think I was a little off my rocker if I began talking to myself.

I never gave it any thought, but I do believe that some of your fluffy ducks that were in line might have waddled off…to a lake…on the other side of the world.

Well, maybe Pearl *was* loosening up just a bit.

Good to know.

I didn't bother to reply to her quip, but instead made my way up the three cement steps to a very immaculate porch. Not even a leaf could be found.

Good housekeeping is very important.

"I'm not saying it isn't, but don't you find it odd that two druids want to be Martha Stewart and play house in a close-knit neighborhood?" I whispered, out of the neighbor's line of sight. "How certain are you that this Jack and Marna didn't have anything to do with Cassie Grier's death?"

As certain as I am that you have a bona fide conspiracy theorist on your hands twenty-four-seven.

Touché.

I slid my left hand inside my jacket pocket, making sure the pouch of powder was easily accessible should I need it to defend myself by deflecting her magic. Technically, it was just enough to allow me to get far enough away from the druid before she could draw any type of focused power should the need arise.

I took a deep breath and rang the doorbell.

You should know that there is a protection spell around the perimeter of this house.

"We thought of that," I murmured, barely moving my lips in case Marna was looking through one of the windows to see who was at her front door. "We added a special evocation to the mix. While there would be a delay in drawing power from the earth, the deferment just wouldn't be as long as usual. It should still afford me time to leave this house and drive away before Marna or Jack had their full power. Thankfully, we only have to worry about one druid."

I'm rather impressed with your—

"Pearl, would you please stop talking? It makes me want to verbally reply every single time." I wondered why it was taking so long for Marna to come to the door. I hadn't seen any movement in the windows, and druids couldn't see through walls or doors. There wasn't any sign of a camera that would suggest she could see who was standing on her front porch, so what could be taking her so long? "Pearl, maybe you should—"

The heavy wooden door swung open before I could suggest that Pearl have a quick peek inside to make sure Marna wasn't getting ready to annihilate me.

You would have wanted me to enter a house without a proper invitation? That is not appropriate etiquette.

I instinctively took a step back and clutched the bag of powder in my fist, barely refraining from throwing it at the older woman who finally peered at me from behind the door with a frown of displeasure.

"We've been expecting you, Tempest Lilura."

It was the *we* part that caught me off guard.

You see, Jack Marna—who I literally just watched leave this house, get into his vehicle, and drive away down the road—was standing behind his wife with green eyes that were practically glowing.

Oh, dear. It seems that we've found ourselves in a bit of a troublesome spot, have we not?

Chapter Eleven

"I'M NOT HERE to stir up any trouble," I managed to get out around the distress caught in my throat. I didn't fear them, necessarily. Facing a Lich who'd basically lost all of her humanity had a tendency to put things into perspective. "I just need a bit of help in solving Cassie Grier's murder."

I do appreciate someone with a backbone of steel.

"Show yourself," Jack demanded of Pearl, the greenish hue of his eyes becoming even brighter. He even took a step forward, closing the distance between him and his wife. "I have no patience for games, familiar."

And I have no tolerance for those with no manners.

"Pearl, don't leave me standing here with my hat in my hand," I warned, automatically tightening my grip on the bag of powder. I didn't want to use my only viable short-term solution that would possibly, most likely, bring about a bad ending to this confrontation. "Remember, the faster I solve Cassie's murder, the quicker Orwin and I can leave town."

Well, when you put it like that...

Sure enough, the sleek white familiar materialized in her haughty manner, appearing as if she'd been walking from behind my right leg. Pearl sat beside my black leather boot with her tail swaying gracefully behind her and her nose lifted in the air to let these druids know she wouldn't be intimidated.

It's a wee bit cold out here. Are you going to invite us in or shall we cause a scene in front of your lovely neighbors?

To say that Jack and Marna were surprised at the offensive tactic Pearl was using was an understatement. Truthfully, so was I. I wasn't foolish enough to believe that we had the upper hand.

In case it has escaped your notice, we do have the upper hand.

"She didn't mean to cause offense," I quickly chimed in, trying my best to soothe over the situation. I wasn't about to resort to blackmailing two druids and have more enemies when I'd already made one with a deranged Lich. "We just have some quick questions that need answering, and then we'll be on our merry way."

"No funny business," Marna warned, stepping back and forcing her husband to do the same. "We simply want to be left in peace."

Their bid sounded heavenly, because I hadn't known peace for over three months.

Don't whine, my dear. It doesn't become you.

Pearl missed my frown when she saw fit to cross the threshold of a druid's home as if it was an everyday occurrence. I quickly followed her, not having a second to spare. We needed answers, and we needed them quick if we were going to save Jamie Lehman from the same fate as that of Cassie Grier.

On the bright side, Pearl had actually referred to me as something else besides *Miss Lilura* or *my dear hexed one*.

That was progress, right?

Progress is only needed to move forward. In case you've forgotten, you'll be gone soon.

"I appreciate your willingness to speak with us," I said without even a hitch in my voice as both Marna and Jack made room for me to enter their home. Pearl was right. Orwin and I would have hit the road last night had Cassie Grier not been murdered. Once we caught the killer, we'd be on our way. "As I said, it's not my intention to cause either of you any problems. I also won't say a word to any of your neighbors about your true identities. I'm only looking for a bit of assistance on what took place in the café last night."

What is that horrid smell?

"What happened last night has already caused my wife and I a bit of trouble, if I'm being honest," Jack replied, the threatening radiance of his eyes subsiding as he led the way into a kitchen that reminded me of my grandmother's when she'd been alive.

Seriously, it was as if I'd been transported back in time.

There were wreaths and ancient pottery pieces sprinkled over the somewhat old-fashioned style counters that I'm pretty sure were still laminate. The yellow walls had been freshly painted, but even the cupboards were out-of-date with white round knobs that had a yellowish tint to them from considerable age.

As for Pearl's comment about an odor, I didn't smell anything out of the ordinary.

How could you miss that...wet stench?

I didn't miss the fact that Marna had given Pearl an offensive sideways glance in regard to the insult. We were definitely getting off on a bad foot, so I quickly dove into the reason for our visit as I took a seat at the kitchen table.

"It's my understanding that the two of you want to retire and live out your days in anonymity." Who was I to judge their decision? Truthfully, I was quite envious of their ability to blend in with the human side of society here in Bedford...raking leaves and doing crossword puzzles in their spare time sounded like heaven. "Please don't think that my presence here today jeopardizes that in any way. I, too, was at the café last night...and we were all just in the wrong place at the wrong time."

You three were in the wrong place at the wrong time. I was right where I was supposed to be, which was watching over my charge during her shift at the café. I'm sure what we can all agree on is that the murder of Cassie Grier threatens to expose all of us if this situation is not resolved properly.

I nodded my head in acknowledgement, waiting for Jack and Marna to do the same. They were staring at each other and talking in some secret code that couples seemed to acquire throughout their years of marriage. I'd never known anything close to that kind of intimacy.

Really? Mr. Cornelia reads your thoughts on a daily basis.

"That's different, and you know it," I replied without thinking, not that it mattered. Jack and Marna could hear every word between me and Pearl. "What I'm trying to say is that while you haven't lived in Bedford for a long time, you've been here long enough to pick up on a few things…such as who would want Cassie Grier dead. I can understand why you would have cloaked the café from anyone taking notice of your presence, but you also gave the killer the ability to escape our detection and possibly get away with murder."

Once again, Jack and Marna exchanged a few glances until they both joined me at the table, signifying that they were willing to help. With that said, their partial acquiescence to the situation wasn't enough for me to take my left hand out of my jacket.

Do you truly not smell that repulsive scent?

Pearl was sitting on the floor next to my chair, her exotic head practically on a swivel. I personally couldn't smell anything but the coffee either Jack or Marna had made this morning.

I'm not fond of coffee, although a spot of tea every now and then is an absolute delight. Cream is what I prefer, but the coffee aroma is not what I'm referring to.

"May I offer you some coffee or tea?" Marna asked,

though more out of politeness than wanting our company.

No doubt that Marna had heard Pearl and assumed that I'd wanted some coffee. I did, but I wasn't going to stay in the company of druids and risk my life, nor was I naïve enough to drink anything brewed up by another spellcaster. I know what you're thinking. The older couple hadn't done a thing to warrant such abject fear on my part, but druids could destroy this house in under ten seconds.

Eight, but who's counting? Carry on.

"No, but thank you for the offer, though." It was time to get down to business. "Jack and Marna, is there anything you can tell me about those individuals who were in the café last night? Did you see or sense anyone who would want Cassie Grier dead?"

Jack had taken off his hat and was holding it in his hands, rubbing the rim as if he weren't quite sure he should get involved. He'd even thinned his lips in disapproval, but that might have been directed toward Pearl for her continual insults concerning their home.

Wouldn't you like to know if the interior of your Jeep had a rather ripe smell?

I wasn't going to get into etiquette with a familiar who probably knew more about propriety than I did, so I waited rather impatiently for either Jack or Marna to reply.

Wise choice.

"You'll be wanting to speak to Tad Whitaker," Jack finally confirmed, setting his hat on his knee before crossing his arms. "He had what you might call a crush on Cassie Grier."

Mr. Whitaker? I don't believe that young man is capable of murder.

"That pour soul," Marna commiserated, as if Tad might not have taken his crush a step too far. She apparently agreed with Pearl's assessment. "Tad has been working up the courage to ask Cassie out for dinner, but he just couldn't bring himself to say anything other than the typical greeting. I don't believe he could have harmed a hair on that girl's head. If you ask me, you'll be wanting to speak with Heather Coyle. Now that woman was mighty envious of Cassie."

I tensed slightly when Marna's grey eyes became rather illuminated, similar to Jack's response to my initial presence. Granted, they would have had to work harder to garner a lot of energy here in the suburbs compared to the country, but even then their combined capabilities were much more powerful than mine.

I don't recall Ms. Coyle saying anything that would indicate she was resentful of Ms. Grier.

"You spend most of your time near your charge, as one should," Jack replied, arching a bushy eyebrow with what seemed to be a hint of respect. "Ms. Coyle has made some snide comments regarding Ms. Grier's career, her car, and even her new apartment. At one point, Ms.

Coyle indicated that she'd put in for the job at an accounting firm where Ms. Grier worked on the other side of town. You see, they had both gone to the same college and obtained their accounting degrees."

A sound came at the kitchen door that had all of us turning our attention to the rectangular cutout inside the wood—a doggie door. It was then that everything began to fall into place, and I immediately stood from my chair. The legs squeaked against the vinyl floor, but that wasn't the cause of every white hair on Pearl's body standing up in alarm. Seriously, her white tail appeared as large as a roll of paper towels.

"And here I thought you never got rattled," I muttered, watching in disbelief as two large brown ears came through the doggie door. Trust me, those weren't dog ears, either. "Pearl, whatever you do…please remember that we're guests here."

In theory, a familiar to a druid could absolutely run circles around a witch's familiar in many aspects. Due to a druid's connection to nature, his or her familiar wasn't a simple cat, dog, or owl. Noooo, druids chose animals from the wild. Seriously, like a bear, lion, or tiger.

What. Is. That?

The large animal—though not quite as big as I'd been expecting from all the stories I'd heard—had finally made its way through the doggie door. Granted, the doggie door was outfitted for the size of a Saint Bernard, but that was neither here nor there.

Marna and Jack must have chosen that particular sized doggie door to accommodate their...extremely large hare? Trust me, the wild animal was way too enormous to be a mere rabbit or its kin. The hare's brown and white fur couldn't hide his wired muscles, and the twitch of his nose made it known that he didn't think Pearl's aroma was all that sweet, either.

We have guests? We have guests, indeed. Rihanna, we have guests!

You know, I've heard of this, Pearl stated in dismay, somehow arching her back even more as a second hare made her way through the doggie door. *A hex can wear off on others, you know. You, my dear hexed one, are very bad luck. I lay the blame for this predicament solely at your feet.*

"Oh, that's just Reginald and Rihanna," Marna replied with a dismissive wave of her hand. "Reggie and Rihanna, please meet Tempest and Pearl. They're from town, and they are only here for information. No need to be rude."

I told you that I caught of whiff of something rancid, Reginald. You never believe me when I tell you anything.

So much for the rude part. If Pearl dug her claws into the vinyl squares any deeper, there were going to be holes left in the floor.

I'd say it's more of a sour odor, my darling. It's been so long since we've been allowed to roam out in the wild that my sense of smell seems to have been affected by the domesticated servants of man.

I managed to scoop Pearl up into my arms right after the rancid comment, but she'd promptly vanished into thin air. The only thing good to come from that conversation told me that their powers had to be drained somewhat from being so far from their natural habitat.

Does that white creature believe that we're impressed by that disappearance act, Reginald?

"Are we going to have a problem?" Jack asked pointedly before grabbing his hat and standing from his seat. It was clear that he was ready to do what was necessary. I had no doubt I'd lose in the end, but Pearl was right when she'd said that we had the upper hand. In no way did Jack or Marna want to give up the private life they'd made here in Bedford. "You came seeking our help, we provided you with the information you needed, and now I suggest you leave."

"I think that's for the best, as well." I sure hoped that Pearl didn't appear out of nowhere to try and attack two hares who could simply squash her with just their tails. I'd never seen her so angry, and that was saying something considering she hadn't been too happy about me and Orwin showing up in Piper's life in the first place. Bottom line, though, was that we'd gotten what we'd come here to get and could be on our way. "I appreciate the information you've given us, and we'll do our best to find Cassie Grier's murderer."

I managed to pass by the two hares, who were still twitching their noses as if they were memorizing my scent...which hopefully was sweeter than Pearl's natural odor.

"May I ask what the feline familiar was referring to with that hex business?" Jack asked, following behind Marna who was currently seeing me out the front door. The cold air was a welcome respite compared to the alternate ending this could have turned out to be, and I was reluctant to stay on the porch any longer than necessary. "How does a witch go about getting cursed?"

"It's a very long story." There was absolutely no way I was going to bring up Ammeline. I had no idea what these druids would do with that type of information, and my life was already chaotic enough. I did want to address something, but I waited until I was on the sidewalk to turn and face them. "Jack and Marna, I don't know why you've chosen to be so very far from where you're most safe and secure in nature. I've had to make some decisions in my life that most wouldn't agree with, but I do want to wish both of you the best in your efforts. I'm sorry that such a tragedy outside of your control threatened to take away all that is important to you. Again, I do wish you both the luck of St. Brigid."

I didn't wait for either druid to reply, for there was no need. Plus, I wanted to get out of Dodge as quickly as I could before things went sideways. I didn't miss that fact that two sets of ears were poking out from behind a covered bush around the side of the house. Those hares weren't the Peter Cottontail type, if you know what I mean.

Rancid? Sour? I don't think so.

"Pearl, what did you do?" I asked, quickly closing the door to enclose us into the safety of my Jeep. The sleek white feline was sitting in the passenger seat as pretty as could be, her chin tilted to the point where her whiskers were easily visible. "Please tell me that we don't have to keep looking over our shoulders the entire rest of the day."

Why would you assume I've done anything?

"Why?" It didn't escape my notice that Marna and Jack were still inside the doorway, waiting for me to pull away from the curb. I quickly started the engine and had the Jeep in drive before whatever Pearl did or left behind was discovered. "Because you disappeared without warning and never returned, leaving me to get out of there all by my lonesome."

It seems to me you fared quite well in that endeavor. As for those two heathens, let's just say I left something behind to teach them the difference between my wonderful scent of roses and what would be considered rancid and sour. There's nothing wrong with teaching a lesson every now and then.

"Pearl, you live here in this town," I reminded her gently, breathing a little easier now that we were headed back to town. "And those hares aren't going anywhere for the foreseeable future. Do you really want to start a war with two giant familiars who have more magical power in their twitchy noses than you have in your entire body?"

My dear hexed one, you will learn through life that magical power has nothing to do with size. A bit of cunning goes a long way in a healthy competition between...associates, shall we say? It's the edge of your wit that cuts the deepest, not the size of the blade.

Pearl was the type of familiar to have a list. You know the kind—a list of people, creatures, or magical beings that have crossed her. No doubt, Orwin and I were somewhere near the bottom whereas those hares had managed to get to the top of the list without even really trying. I shuddered to think the damage she could do if she really set her mind to it. From what I remember from my studies, crypt cats usually appeared quite different than Pearl, but their capabilities were renowned. They could wither the most powerful among us.

Another highway, another town, and another mystery were sounding better and better.

"Pearl, it's time to take your rose-smelling...tail...to the police station and check up on your temporary ward's safety." Jamie Lehman's life was hanging in the balance, but I now had some substantial information to go on thanks to two reclusive druids. "I'm going to call Orwin and Piper to see who they've been able to talk to this morning. All roads point toward either Tad or Heather, and we're running out of time."

Time meaning minutes or hours that could very well avoid my vision of Jamie Lehman's cold and lonely death in the parking lot of the mall.

Well, when you put it like that...

Chapter Twelve

"WHAT DO YOU mean, Heather called in sick?" I asked, having just pulled in front of Tad Whitaker's apartment building. I wasn't sure what kind of vehicle he drove, so I'd have to go inside the building to see if he was even home. "Did you swing by her place to see if she was telling the truth? She could still be shaken by what took place last night. Have Piper take her some soup. That should at least get you through her door."

I tried to put myself in Heather's shoes for a moment. If I were innocent of any wrongdoing, and regardless of whatever tension there had been over a job, losing someone who had been a part of my life would take an emotional toll. I wouldn't have wanted to go in to work, either.

"We swung by Heather's studio apartment. She wasn't home," Orwin replied, sounding a bit better in the nasal department. He probably stopped at one of those car wash places to vacuum out Piper's vehicle. He was very thorough like that. "We were able to speak with

Vickie, but she wasn't of any help. She said Cassie had no enemies, no boyfriends, and wasn't the type of person anyone would want to see dead."

"Basically, Vickie painted a picture of Cassie with a golden halo." I'd seen death erase far too many truths while wiping out almost every offense the victim had ever caused in his or her life. It was just the way of things, and it certainly didn't help in our quest to solve a murder. "Anything she says isn't going to help us, so move on to the next person on your list. Maybe Heather didn't want to be alone last night and slept at one of her other friend's places."

I'd already given Orwin and Piper the rundown on my visit with Marna and Jack, leaving out the fact that Pearl might have started a mini turf war between her and the hares. If all worked out, Orwin and I would be on our way out of town by this evening, long before we joined those furry hares at the top of Pearl's list.

"Lou, where did you say you were going next now that you can't talk to Jamie yet?" Piper asked, her voice coming across loud and clear. Orwin had me on speaker phone, so I'd been very careful to limit Pearl's involvement in the recount of my story. "You should know that Tad texted me a bit ago. He said he had to go in to the café early, and he wondered if I'd be willing to start my shift at one o'clock due to some stomach virus hitting the morning crew."

I'd just wasted around ten minutes driving through

town to the south side, but that was neither here nor there. As long as Pearl remained vigilant in her task with making sure Jamie Lehman was safe, we still had time to bring the killer to justice.

I figured we had another fifteen hours before the twenty-four-hour period from when my visions usually came true. With that said, I could distinctly recall Jamie Lehman being killed in broad daylight. The day had been overcast, similar to what it was now. Going on that assumption, we most likely only had seven or eight hours left to prevent another murder.

"It looks like I'm heading back to the café. Where are you two at now?"

"Turns out that John Cooper lives in the same apartment building as Heather Coyle. He was the guy on his computer near that one outlet. His table was too far away from me to get a read on him last night, though."

"I remember," I replied, looking over my shoulder as I backed out of the parking slot I'd claimed. "Mr. Cooper was the one grappling with his phone, no doubt trying to record anything of interest to post to social media."

What was wrong with society these days?

People wanted their fifteen minutes of fame rather than calling 911 in order to help save the victim.

It wasn't that I didn't understand the benefits of social media.

I was twenty-eight years old and had used all the

social media platforms before my run-in with Ammeline. I'd posted pictures of my morning coffee or the sunrise to share the start of the day with my friends. Anything I found interesting or funny would be shared, and then so on and so forth.

Unfortunately, having spent the last three months away from the constant daily streaming allowed me to see things in a new light.

Social media had been intended to bring those apart closer. Instead, it allowed people to hide behind their computers, falsify their lives in a positive light, and to give their opinion on matters that were normally reserved for private conversations amongst family and friends.

The new normal consisted of arguing positions on whether a dress was actually a certain color, recording and posting videos of crimes online instead of assisting the victims, and following whatever stunt a Hollywood actor or actress had done in order to gain more followers.

The only thing Orwin and I used social media for these days was to help solve mysteries, and maybe try to keep tabs on family members we'd rather avoid.

I guess I hadn't noticed it before, but it was almost as if we'd lived in some apocalyptic setting, which technically wasn't far from the case. After all, we were fighting against the insanity of a Lich who could destroy our world with just a tap of her cane.

"Lou? You there?"

"Yeah, yeah," I replied, refocusing my thoughts on

one Tad Whitaker. I flipped my turn signal on in the direction of town. Since I was using the Bluetooth speaker to hold this conversation, no doubt the ticking noise from my blinker was echoing through the line. "I'm heading back into town now. I should be at the café in around four minutes. I'll talk with Tad while you see if John Cooper saw anything of interest. Who knows? Maybe he caught something on video and posted it to social media. You should check that out before talking to him."

"I did that when you were having your early morning nap." Orwin was nothing if not efficient, which was why his next statement didn't surprise me in the least. And I lay the sole responsibility at Pearl's paws. "Hey, you should know that I've also booked us a room in Kecksburg. Seeing as we're so close, I thought we should check it out. Good luck with Tad!"

Orwin was the first to disconnect, most likely not wanting to hear my thoughts on the whole UFO conspiracy thing. It was true that I usually had a couple of days in between visions, but I certainly didn't have time to spend an hour—let alone twenty-four hours—in Kecksburg, Pennsylvania.

I guess I could leave Orwin there overnight if I decided to close on the Custom Coach deal. The dealership can have it delivered to Pittsburgh with two days' notice, but I'd have to make my decision soon.

I blamed Pearl for the foreseeable side trip in my near

future.

I had already accepted that there was a chance one of my visions could lead us to Nevada, landing us square within walking distance from Area 51. Of course, there was a valid reason for that—what better place for supernatural beings to live their lives than in a place where tourists expected odd people and occurrences?

On a side note, Orwin hadn't disconnected fast enough to prevent me from hearing Piper speak up to let me know that Tad was basically a good guy. I'm sure he was, but even the nicest of men could be turned by an unhealthy obsession with someone.

Had Tad asked Cassie out last night as she was walking toward the restroom? If she'd turned him down, would he have been so enraged as to follow her inside one of the stalls and stab her to death?

I'm assuming there would have been blood all over the boy were your scenario even remotely correct. Unless Mr. Whitaker had enough time to change his white work shirt, of course.

I barely avoided steering into an oncoming vehicle in reaction to Pearl's abrupt visit, who'd once again materialized in the passenger seat as if I were used to such comings and goings. I wasn't. I had no familiar, and I sure wasn't inclined to get one after meeting her.

"Pearl, stop that! You're going to get us both killed."

It's not like I can knock, Miss Lilura.

"Well, figure something out or I'll take you back to those hares and leave you at their mercy." Once my heartrate settled a bit, anger and fear began to settle in. Did Pearl not understand the severity of my vision? She'd seen it firsthand. "Pearl, Jamie Lehman's life is depending on us to keep her safe. I *saw* her die in that parking lot. We can't take the chance that I missed something."

I know exactly what you saw, and how dare you assume that I would put an innocent life in danger? I'm offended that you would even think such a thing, Miss Lilura.

"Then why are you here with me instead of Jamie?" I turned onto the main thoroughfare in town, searching for a parking spot near the café. It was now mid-morning. Everyone and their mother wanted to get their caffeine fix. Even though I was in desperate need of some myself, I came very close to driving to the police station instead of the café. "Is she still with Detective Jones?"

If you'd knock that massive chip off your shoulder, lovey, I might be able to get a word in edgewise.

I began my count to ten, hoping to achieve even an ounce of patience.

Now, isn't that better? I can now catch you up to speed on the last twenty minutes. Ms. Lehman has been called in to the café. The morning manager—

"Came down with the flu," I said, finishing Pearl's appraisal of the situation. It looked as if the café was definitely my destination. "I just spoke with Orwin and Piper. Tad was called in to work, as well. Piper was asked to go in one hour early. Is Jamie at the café now? We can—"

As snug as a bug in a rug.

Well, didn't that just up my guilt meter. I'd jumped on Pearl without allowing her to tell me that she'd seen through her mission to keep Jamie Lehman safe.

No need to apologize. We're all on edge. I suggest you take advantage of this opportunity, seeing as you have three suspects corralled into one place.

"Three?"

Pearl didn't answer me.

A quick glance at the passenger seat told me that she'd vanished into thin air, most likely back to the café where Jamie Lehman was now filling in during the morning shift. Piper's familiar had a tendency to leave out information that would be beneficial in times like these, but I'd already figured out who one of the individuals she'd been referring to was based on the Land Rover parked directly in front of the café.

We'd ruled Knox Emeric out of the suspect pool, but I still had an inherent sense that he was withholding critical information. It looked as if Pearl felt the same. Maybe I should have had her listen in on those interviews this morning.

I was lucky that someone was pulling out of a parking spot across the street or else I would have had to use the parking lot of the nearby mall. I managed to quickly make my way across the street after hitting the lock button on the key fob, wishing Orwin would hurry up in his questioning of John Cooper. Pearl might be able to get a read on magical beings, but only Orwin had the ability to read human thoughts.

The delicious aroma of coffee washed over me the moment I opened the door, causing the bell above my head to chime at my arrival. No one bothered to look my way with the exception of Knox Emeric. He was always on alert...or so it seemed.

He was sitting at the same table he'd occupied last night, enjoying a cup of coffee and what looked to be some type of breakfast sandwich. His warm gaze rested on me before he nodded slightly in greeting. I resisted the urge to walk over to him.

Stop being distracted by the big bad wolf, my dear Red Riding Hood. We have work to do, and Grandma's house isn't on the agenda.

Sure enough, Pearl was strolling toward me from behind the counter as if I'd been about to make a horrible decision. I hadn't been going to join Knox at his table for the heck of it, but to ask about his meeting with Detective Jones. That was considered work, in my opinion. Hadn't Pearl herself insinuated that there were three suspects in the coffee shop?

Mr. Emeric can wait, but you only have a few moments to speak to those young girls ordering vanilla nonfat lattes up at the counter. They have class at the college in thirty minutes, although the brunette is attempting to talk the redhead into skipping today's lecture.

The names of the two nineteen-year-olds had been listed last on our list simply due to the process of elimination. It wasn't that I believed someone so young couldn't commit such a horrible crime as murder, but they had the least likely motive to kill Cassie Grier—which simply wasn't there.

Aren't those mysteries on television written that way on purpose? Never assume, Miss Lilura.

This wasn't *Murder, She Wrote*, and I wasn't human. What I had discerned was that the three suspects Pearl had mentioned earlier consisted of Tad and these two college girls. Personally, I still had Knox on the reserve list, but that was because I didn't trust him or his nature.

That's very wise, dear. Now move your fanny out of the way. You're blocking someone's entrance, so I suggest you join the others in ordering their beloved caffeinated beverages. I suggest tea, though. The calming properties far outweigh the...

Pearl continued to talk about tea as I made my way to the short line, bringing myself to stand directly behind Emma Day and Sophia Moore. The nineteen-year-old girls were rather quiet, and I noticed that Emma kept glancing toward the restroom with unease. Honestly, I wasn't so sure I would have come back to this café if I were them. At least, not for quite a while.

The owner of the café is in the back office on the phone trying to do damage control. Looking at all these people, I don't believe she has a thing to worry about. Morbid curiosity is a thing, you know.

The café *was* pretty crowded, and I'd also noticed a local media van down the street when I was parking the

Jeep. The cameraman was probably trying to get the entirety of the café's name in the shot while the reporter gave his or her account of the ongoing investigation.

"I don't know why you wanted to come back here," Emma muttered to her friend, still waiting for the man in front of her to finish his order. She wrapped her arms around her waist as she shot Sophia a frustrated glance. "It just feels wrong somehow."

"I heard that Michael Pierce was going to be here," Sophia commented with what sounded like excitement. She scanned the patrons, her frown clearly indicating that she couldn't find this Mr. Pierce she'd mentioned. "He might interview us if we can somehow drop a hint to let him know we were here last night when *it* happened."

Michael Pierce is the reporter outside, if you'd like to know. He's been here for quite a while, from my understanding. I personally don't see all the fuss about the man's appearance. The fake tan he's sporting makes him look like he used some of your foundation.

"I don't want to be on television, and neither should you." Emma leaned in close toward her friend. "Whoever killed that woman is still out there somewhere. Doesn't that worry you?"

Sophia was prevented from answering when the man at the cash register moved out of their way, sliding his credit card back into his wallet and taking a spot near the pickup counter. It sounded horrible, but I wasn't so much worried about the killer than I was the fact that my tinted moisturizer had apparently left a line along the underside of my jaw.

Left side, dear. Left side.

"I'd be worried about that, too," I replied softly to Emma after she'd place her order of a nonfat vanilla latte. I finally lowered my hand to my side. If I did look like a pumpkin head from the tinted moisturizer, there wasn't a thing I could do about it now. "A few of these people look familiar, and any one of them could have followed that poor woman to the restroom. I told Detective Jones all I know, but I didn't know the victim. Did you?"

"No, I didn't know her," Emma replied, exchanging worried looks with Sophia. They were both now scanning the faces of the patrons inside the café, Michael Pierce easily forgotten. "Hey. Wasn't that guy here last night?"

That wasn't very nice of you to veer their suspicions toward Mr. Emeric. From the look on his face, he's realized what you've done.

It hadn't been a nice thing to do, but I pushed the guilt aside and focused on my objective. I'd found over the last three months that distraction inevitably led to people letting things slip. I could definitely get these two girls to talk.

"He *was* one of the people here last night," Sophia confirmed with barely a whisper, pushing Emma toward the pickup counter now that they'd placed and paid for their orders. A little bit of fear made one cautious, so I didn't feel too much remorse. "I didn't know the woman, but I had seen her around town a time or two with Vickie."

I give you credit, oh mighty hexed one. Very well done.

"Vickie?" I asked, already knowing that was one of the names of the women who had been friends with Cassie Grier.

As for Pearl's compliment, that was high praise from the white feline.

"Vickie Traynor," Sophia explained, keeping close tabs on Knox. Okay. Maybe I did feel a little bit guilty for throwing him under the bus. "She works at the veterinarian clinic where we take our dog. She's a real nice lady."

I thought I caught the whiff of wet dog. Horrible odor, just horrible!

"What about the other woman they were with last night?" I asked, hoping to keep the conversation going. I quickly ordered a plain black coffee and handed over a crumbled five-dollar bill I had in my coat pocket. I'd found it best not to carry a purse, seeing that extra baggage slowed down my movements whenever I needed to protect myself…or run. "Did you know her?"

Emma might have been the quiet one, but she was the more astute of the two. She regarded me carefully before taking a step back, clearly noting that I was doing more than just making small talk. Tad Whitaker was in the process of making their drinks, but Emma wasn't focused on him at all.

"Oh, you're talking about Megan Kirk," Sophia said, still carrying on the conversation while keeping a wary eye on Knox. "I don't know her either, other than that she hangs around Heather all the time. Megan and Cassie were in a heated argument about something outside of the café last night, but they seemed to make up by the time they sat down. I told that to the detective, but I didn't want him to think I was suggesting anything. I wasn't. Hey, do you think..."

I tuned Sophia out for just a moment while I went over that new tidbit of information. Megan and Cassie had been in a heated argument before they came into the café? I needed to call Orwin and Piper to have them talk with Megan as soon as possible.

That won't be necessary, dear. Megan Kirk just walked into the café. It seems as if the café is just a gathering place for all our suspects, doesn't it?

Chapter Thirteen

"...APPRECIATE YOU MEETING me here," Detective Jones said after he'd joined Megan at a table next to the pickup counter. As I said before, the café was quite crowded. I took my time choosing the white packets of sugar and tearing off the top portion. "I wanted to go back over the events of last night with you."

You should know that you've captured Detective Jones' interest. Not in the romantic way either, but more in a suspicious manner where he's trying to figure out why you're here...back at the scene of the crime.

"Anything I can do to help catch Cassie's killer," Megan replied politely, setting her small purse on her lap with what appeared to be an odd smile that didn't quite reach her eyes. I'm pretty sure it had to do with the fact that she was back in a place that surely brought back memories of what she'd discovered in the women's restroom. Either that or she was frightened that Detective Jones would figure out that she had something to do with Cassie Grier's murder. Her eyes were still rather bloodshot from grief. "It's just all so horrible. I mean, who could have done such a horrible thing?"

I must give Detective Jones' credit in having certain suspects meet him back at the scene of the crime. If I were ever guilty of murder, such a tactic might cause me to have a misstep.

I doubted that anything or anyone would cause Pearl to confess to a crime...even the murder of a wayward pharaoh.

You're right, of course, but it was my way of giving the good detective his due. I was not speculating on anyone's lack of character or crimes from their past.

"What can I get you, Ms. Kirk?" Detective Jones asked, obviously deciding to make Megan a bit more comfortable by plying her with a caffeine beverage.

You're going to stir a hole right through that cup if you aren't careful, Nancy Drew.

I focused on adding some half and half to my already sweetened coffee, hoping that Detective Jones would walk right past me to the cash register. My next step was to find a table where I could hear their upcoming conversation.

"I remember you, puffball."

Puffball? Just who do you think you are? What are you doing? What—stop. Cease this minute! Don't you dare—

I didn't have to turn around to know that Detective Jones was speaking to Pearl and most likely kneeling to give her a small rub down her back or an itch behind her ear. The small—definitely unwelcomed from the familiar's reaction—diversion allowed me to quickly take my coffee and move to a spot off to the side.

Maybe Pearl was right about bad luck rubbing off from the hex. There was not one table available. I'd wanted to sit close enough to Megan's table to hear what she had to say to Detective Jones, but that wasn't going to happen. A quick sweep of the café confirmed my suspicion that I was out luck, but apparently, I did have one option available to me—Knox Emeric was leaning back against his chair with a crooked smile across his lips. It was almost as if he found my plight amusing.

The chair in front of him was empty.

I had a decision to make—join Knox Emeric at his table to remain in the café or leave.

"Jill with a large caramel macchiato," Tad called out, reminding me that there was more work to be done.

The decision had been taken out of my hands.

Jamie Lehman was still inside the café, along with too many suspects who could be the guilty party in the vision I had regarding her death. I'd have to put aside my suspicion of Knox Emeric long enough to make sure Jamie Lehman was safe for the time being.

I had just been about to walk over to Knox's table when my phone rang. I didn't even have to look at the display to know that it was Orwin. He was the only one who ever called me, especially since I hadn't returned any of my former friends' calls in the last three months.

"Make it quick," I murmured, walking around two ladies who were making their way to the line behind

Detective Jones. His gaze was still on me, but I'd already answered his follow-up questions last night. That was probably the only reason that Orwin and I hadn't been called into the station today. "I'm at the café, and let me just say that there's a lot going on here. You and Piper might want to make your way over here as soon as you can."

"Did you know that Megan Kirk and Cassie Grier had an argument right before they went into the café last night?" Orwin asked before continuing on in the same breath and not giving me time to answer. "Well, they did, and it was a doozy. According to Heather, the two women were fighting over a man. Are you ready for this? The man they were fighting over was none other than Tad Whitaker."

Poor Tad. He didn't even know that Cassie returned his feelings, did he?

Pearl sashayed past me with her tail swaying behind her, but she didn't stroll toward Knox Emeric. Instead, she veered off to head down the small hallway that led to the restrooms and the double doors that led to the storage and office area.

Our dear Jamie just went back to speak with her manager. As you've said time and again, she shouldn't be left alone. I'll also use the bit of privacy offered to me to cleanse this dog smell that Detective Jones saw fit to leave on practically every single hair on my body. My opinion of that man has drastically changed. I'd originally thought of him as a cat person. Alas, not everyone is perfect.

"Come to the café," I advised Orwin, pasting a smile on my face when I realized that Knox Emeric was still watching me rather closely. I hope the man couldn't read lips. "Without the druids cloaking everyone's thoughts, you should be able to narrow down the suspect pool drastically with who is in here at the moment."

"We'll be there in ten minutes or less."

I disconnected the call and shoved my phone back into my coat pocket. One would think someone would have left the café by now, leaving an open table. No such luck. It appeared that murder was good for business.

"I'm surprised you haven't left town, Mr. Emeric." I pulled the chair out from the table a bit, carefully setting down my coffee before making myself comfortable. "Did your conversation with Detective Jones not go well?"

"It went fine, thank you." Knox studied me while rubbing his five o'clock shadow before slowly leaning forward and placing his elbows on the table. It was as if he'd made some internal decision, and he was debating on whether or not to clue me in on his inner battle. Of course, my assumption was before he gave me a lopsided grin. "I haven't decided if you like the coffee here or you're just stalking me."

Was he flirting with me?

"It could be the other way around," I countered with a returned smile, wrapping my hand around the coffee cup. The warmth kept me grounded and focused on keeping my wits about me. I didn't have time for personal relationships, and Knox Emeric wasn't even my type. "First the gas station, then this café, not to mention the motel. Now we're back at the scene of the crime, and I still haven't quite figured out why you'd pick such a small town as Bedford, Pennsylvania, to do an overnight. After all, Wi-Fi is available in other places."

"I'll give you the real reason I'm here, if you tell me why you're trying so hard to solve Cassie Grier's murder."

I'd thought I'd thrown Knox off balance long enough for me to take a sip of my coffee.

I was wrong.

I'd been played, but not without seeing one of his cards. I was accurate in guessing that he'd been watching me more closely than just a casual observer. One question stood out amongst the others—just who exactly was Knox Emeric?

"Why would you think I would be so foolish as to chase after a killer when Detective Jones seems like he's doing such a fine job?" I managed to ask after setting my cup back down on the table. "I'm simply in town visiting a friend of mine, but I'd bet money that isn't the reason you're here."

Had Ammeline sent one of her lackeys to monitor my movements? Did she know that I was looking for a way to break the hex she'd cursed me with or the fact that I was hunting for her lair? If the cane she carried with her did encompass the power of her immortality, then I had no choice but to locate them both and attempt to end this wretched existence she'd left me alive to live.

I wanted my life back.

"You and your friend didn't stay long at the hotel last night." Knox's golden eyes remained focused on me, studying every expression that crossed my face. Teaching college students had taught me never to let them see my frustration, and I utilized that talent now. "Neither did I, actually."

Was Knox admitting that he'd followed Orwin, Piper, and me to Jamie Lehman's house? No, Orwin would have noticed if we weren't alone outside the house. As for Pearl, she'd done a perimeter check once every hour to make sure we hadn't missed anything.

Knox Emeric was baiting me once again to reveal more information than he seemed willing to give. Was he a warlock? Was he a druid? I didn't get a sense that he was either, but I was at a loss as to the reason he was interested in my movements. That left Ammeline as the reason he was here.

Was Knox waiting for me to mention the hex?

Well, he could wait a century because that wasn't going to happen.

"Our friend was upset about what happened here last night, so we ended up staying at her place to keep her company." I observed every fleck in Knox's golden eyes for any sign that he knew the truth to the contrary. He didn't. He was fishing without any bait, which meant I was going to swim right by his hook into open waters. "I'm sorry to hear that the bed at the motel wasn't up to your standards."

Knox smiled, and I mean…he really smiled. His parents had obviously spent a great deal of money at the orthodontist when he was a young boy. His teeth were sparkling white and as close to perfect as I'd ever seen.

He did know something, but it wasn't that I'd been keeping tabs on Jamie Lehman.

Remember when I said that I wasn't much of a patient person? Well, I also had an aversion to being kept in the dark.

"I can see I need to earn a bit of that trust you keep so close to your chest, so I'll go first." Knox lifted his coffee cup and pointed it in the direction of the cash register. "Tad Whitaker had a crush on Cassie Grier, and Megan Kirk found out about it. The two women got into an argument late yesterday afternoon about the fact that Cassie was considering approaching him first and asking him out to dinner. It seems as if Megan wanted the young man all to herself. Heather Coyle lost out on a job at one of the most coveted accounting firms to Cassie. Vickie Traynor is the peacemaker of the four, but she had her own reasons for not liking Cassie after the two had a disagreement about Heather's right to be upset. Sides were taken, and Heather was friends with Megan and Vickie long before Cassie into the picture."

I remained silent throughout Knox's observations, noting that he'd found out something about Vickie that we'd overlooked. With that said, I'd found that sometimes information was discovered at the most random times and from the oddest places...people included. What I wanted to know was why Knox had gathered this information if he was just truly a wayward traveler. It made no sense, but I wasn't one to turn down a source.

"And the other witnesses who were here last night?" I asked, purposefully taking another sip of coffee as if we were having a normal conversation. "Did any of them have motive to want Cassie Grier dead?"

"Only one." Knox casually leaned back in his chair. It wasn't until after he'd given me a name and a motive that I realized he'd put space between us for a reason. "Piper Allifair. I mean, it was Cassie Grier who discovered that Piper had a secret that could expose her family for what they truly are—witches. But you already know that, don't you?"

Chapter Fourteen

"WHO ARE YOU?"

Those three words fell off my lips before I could stop them.

Knox Emeric wasn't an ordinary human, and if he was...well, my kind could very well be in real trouble if he wished to out all of us. I'm not talking about Ammeline level trouble, but trouble nonetheless.

Is there a problem out here?

"I'm just a friend who wants to help," Knox replied softly, never once breaking the connection of our gaze. He didn't even startle at Pearl's voice, and that alone told me far more than he had in the last five minutes. "I'm not the bad guy here, Lou."

Did someone mention Piper? Is there something I should know?

I was saved from having to answer Knox, because not for one second did I believe this man had any interest in friendship. It was more believable that Ammeline had sent him to keep an eye on me, letting me go through life trying to save people from death itself than allow me time to figure out how to get rid of this curse.

Was this Ammeline's way of making sure that no one would help me? If Knox was willing to expose Piper and her family, what other lengths would he go to for Ammeline?

Are you saying that Ammeline sent this man to distract you? Oh, I don't believe that for a second. Did someone slip something into your coffee, lovey?

"Ms. Lilura, I was hoping you'd have a second to speak with me." As I said, my conversation with Knox had been interrupted. Unfortunately, it was by Detective Jones. He was apparently done following up with Megan Kirk and had set his sights on me. "Mr. Emeric, I didn't expect to see you nor did I know that the two of you are friends."

Friends might be a bit of a stretch. How have you managed to alienate a—

"More like acquaintances," I corrected, taking this opportunity to put some much-needed space between me and Knox Emeric. Now that the druids weren't cloaking the area, Orwin would be able to get a better read on the man other than he didn't like the price of gas in the state of Pennsylvania. I stood and gave Detective Jones my full attention. "What can I help you with, Detective Jones?"

If Knox Emeric thought I would reveal what he knew about Piper to the police, he was sorely mistaken.

Reveal? About Piper? Good gracious, you make it sound like he suggested Piper would have motive to kill Cassie Grier!

That had basically been the gist of it, but Knox Emeric was wrong. Piper didn't kill Cassie, and I wasn't all that sure that he was telling me the truth regarding Cassie finding out about Piper's lineage.

I leave you alone for five minutes—five minutes—and my sweet Piper is now a suspect in a murder. You fix this, Miss Lilura, or I won't be held accountable for my actions.

Great. Now I had Pearl mad at me. This day was certainly shaping up to be a long one, and it wasn't even noon yet.

Noon is how long you have to fix this mess you've gotten my charge into, and also how long you have to leave town. I was snookered into the excitement of solving a mystery, and I lapsed in my responsibility. Shame on me.

"I wanted to go over one more time your statement regarding those individuals you saw going in and out of the restrooms," Detective Jones said as he led the way back to the table where he'd left his coffee. Megan Kirk was nowhere in sight, which did cause me to be a bit uncomfortable. Had Megan left by the front door or had she somehow walked toward the back office where Jamie Lehman had gone to speak to the owner of the café? Had Cassie shared her suspicions of Piper with the others? "You mentioned that you didn't see anyone else enter the women's restroom after Cassie Grier walked by your table."

Megan Kirk left through the front door. Now, carry on with this interview and fix this mess you've gotten my sweet Piper mixed up in and...wait just a magical minute. What did you just say about suspicions? You're not telling me that Cassie knew—

"No," I revised, answering Detective Jones while I took the seat that Megan had vacated. Pearl was already worked up over Piper being a suspect, and I had no time to ease her concerns over the other matter. "I was facing the door, so I didn't notice anyone else walking in the direction of the restroom. If someone from behind the counter needed to go back toward the restroom or the back office, I'm not sure I would have seen them."

You better make time to ease my concerns if this is regarding Piper's lineage. Are we talking about one or two humans…or a complete outage that could put our entire kind in peril? I think I'm having a hot flash. Is this what anxiety feels like? Because I have to tell you that I'm not a fan of it.

I wish I could have answered Pearl, because I would have given myself a bit of reassurance. Unfortunately, I had no idea what information Cassie may or may not have been privy to before her death.

Unfortunately, we may never know…and that might actually be in our favor.

Oh, this situation is worse than I thought. I just realized that I've become complacent in my task to keep Piper safe from harm. Nothing ever happens here in Bedford. Could it be? Could it be that I've lost my edge?

Sure enough, a quick glance behind me showed that Pearl was pacing back and forth in front of the entrance in her flurry of panic. Anyone looking would just assume the white pristine cat was a bit restless, but that would be an understatement.

How good are you at casting spells? I'm not talking about the small enchantments that could make your life easier, but more of the monumental ones that could erase the memories of an entire town.

I wasn't going to make any hasty decisions. It was best I concentrate on the conversation at hand until Orwin and Piper walked through the door. Orwin would be able to figure out what every individual in this café was thinking in a matter of minutes.

As for the investigation, Detective Jones was well aware that Knox Emeric had been in the men's restroom at the time of Cassie Grier's murder. He would have also been told that Piper had been the barista making the various drinks and had been working there for at least forty minutes without leaving her station. I'm pretty sure I hadn't put anyone else in the crosshairs of Detective Jones who hadn't already been there.

Well, someone might very well have put the entire supernatural realm in the crosshairs of every human. Where did Knox Emeric get this kind of information? I, for one, would like to know how.

That was a very good question, but I already had the detective looking at me with suspicion due to me appearing somewhat distracted…which I was. I could only deal with one problem at a time.

A problem? You consider me a problem, Miss Lilura?

I despised when Pearl resorted to my surname, but it

was better to have her direct her anger at me than a human.

"I was also in line for a while and focused on ordering my drink," I reminded Detective Jones, having gone over the events of last night numerous times. Anyone could have walked behind me to the restroom, had enough time to murder Cassie Grier, and make it back to their table before I'd joined Orwin…who no doubt would have been on his laptop doing some research on my predicament. "I'm not sure how much time passed from the time I was in line to when I went back to my table. You really should ask those women who were here with Cassie. They were all sitting down at the table while I was in line for coffee."

My memories are becoming clearer about last night. I was so focused on you and your alien hunter that I wasn't paying attention to the comings and goings from the restrooms.

The detective's ability to trust anyone at this stage of the investigation was practically nonexistent. I couldn't say that I blamed him. He didn't believe he was getting the entire truth from Cassie's so-called group of friends. I didn't think they were being completely honest with him, either.

Miss Lilura, I apologize. I realize now that you had nothing to do with my complacency, and I take full responsibility.

Pearl was giving me whiplash with her belief on who was at fault, but she'd soon come to accept that no one could have prevented Cassie Grier from being murdered.

Just as it was becoming more and more difficult in this day and age to keep the magical realm of the supernatural hidden from human society.

"Didn't you say that you were here visiting a friend?" Detective Jones asked, clearly changing the subject to focus on me and my motives. This wasn't such a good turn of events, but I was saved when Orwin and Piper came through the front door of the café. "What a coincidence."

"Not really," I replied with a smile, making sure I appeared relaxed under his watchful gaze. I had my back to Knox Emeric, but I'd done so on purpose. He wouldn't try anything in a room full of witnesses, and I didn't want him to see my reactions when speaking with Detective Jones. "Orwin and I are getting ready to leave town, and he'd wanted to spend some time with Piper before we left."

...believe that Cassie may have known that you and your family are witches. We must speak with your father, posthaste. There is no time to waste, so you must inform Ms. Lehman that you cannot work today. I'll escort you to the family homestead while we allow Miss Lilura and Mr. Cornelu to fulfil whatever obligations they feel they have here. After we speak with your parents, we can then...

Pearl continued to fill Piper in on everything that had occurred within the last ten minutes, but to anyone looking...Piper was just loving on her cat. No one had questioned Pearl's appearance at the café without her rightful owner, which told me that she was a regular here.

"Lou, is everything okay?" Orwin asked, most likely being inundated with unwanted thoughts from every patron within a six-foot distance. He hid his frustration well, and I also recognized that he'd done so for the past three months. Pearl was all I could handle, and Orwin dealt with a lot more than one familiar on a daily basis. "Detective Jones, has something happened in the case?"

…what are you doing? Piper Faye Allifair, come back here right this minute.

"Unfortunately, there have been no new developments." Detective Jones scooted over so that Orwin had room to sit in the booth side. The table we were at was one of those half booths with chairs on the outer side of the table. "Have a seat, Mr. Cornelia. I was just asking Ms. Lilura if she could remember anything from last night that she may have forgotten to mention."

I'm too old for this.

It wasn't like Orwin could decline Detective Jones' offer. What we really needed to happen was for Orwin to walk past Emma and Sophia, as well as stand near Tad in order to find out what each and every one of them were thinking.

As for Pearl, she'd meekly—and I used that word mildly—trailed behind Piper as the blonde made her way over to the chair next to me. Every other table was still occupied, but again, I didn't want to turn around to find Knox Emeric staring in my direction.

Meek? Your internal dictionary could use a little updating, oh mighty hexed one. I'm not, nor have I ever been, meek.

"Isn't that one of Cassie Grier's friends?" Orwin asked, having looked in the direction of the front entrance when the bell chimed. I couldn't help myself. I peered over my shoulder, catching a glimpse of Heather, who'd apparently met Megan outside of the café. "I do find it surprising that they would want to come here for coffee after what happened last night."

Once again, Detective Jones has surprised me with such insight into a witness' mind. Either Ms. Coyle is much better at applying her makeup than you are, Miss Lilura, or she doesn't appear to be that upset about the passing of her dear friend.

Orwin's prompt was enough to get Detective Jones to mutter a quick apology as he stood up to make his way over to the women. My guess was that he'd had Megan meeting him here, and then decided to have Heather do the same.

Would the detective's tactics work?

Was it possible that Megan or Heather was the killer? Or even both?

I admire the man's tenacity, although I don't quite forgive him for his penchant for dogs, of all creatures. Now, back to business. My sweet Piper should be our main concern.

"Neither one of those women murdered Cassie Grier," Orwin replied once Detective Jones was out of earshot. He leaned forward with his phone in hand, giving Pearl an odd look that said she'd lost him with her part of the conversation. "I passed both Heather and

Megan to come inside the café, and they had nothing to do with Cassie's murder. Vickie is in the clear, too."

That narrows the suspect pool, but it doesn't take care of the most important matter at hand.

"I'm telling you that Tad didn't murder Cassie," Piper piped in, leaning her elbows on the table as well. If Knox Emeric was keeping an eye on me, as I suspected he was, he'd surely see three people conspiring to keep a secret. "Lou, what has Pearl so concerned about us being outed as…you know?"

Mr. Emeric had the audacity to suggest that you, my sweet Piper, had motive to kill Cassie Grier.

Orwin grabbed one of those thin paper napkins, but he was too late to catch his sneeze.

"I don't understand," Piper whispered, leaning closer to me at the exact moment I could sense that Orwin had caught something of interest from someone close by. "Why would that man think that I could do something so horrible? He doesn't even know me."

I say we all put down our teacups and do what has to be done—eviscerate the man.

Chapter Fifteen

"D ID SHE JUST use the word *eviscerate*?" Orwin's dark gaze swung to Detective Jones, who was still speaking with Heather and Megan. "Lou, this has gotten to a whole new level. We're not equipped for dealing with that amount of violence, in case you hadn't noticed."

I'm not seeing the problem here. We can even enjoy a hot cup of tea afterward.

"We are not eviscerating anyone." I was completely losing control of this conversation. It didn't help that Detective Jones would more than likely want his table back. "Piper, Knox Emeric wasn't suggesting that he believes you killed Cassie. He was just pointing out..."

You can't win this one, my dear hexed one. Knox Emeric must be eliminated.

"I'm surrounded by the certifiably insane," Orwin muttered, rubbing the bridge of his nose before putting his glasses back in place. He looked at me as if I could fix our current situation. "You're going to do something, right?"

You better be referring to our current predicament, Mr. Cornelia.

"Knox Emeric *was* suggesting that I could murder someone in cold blood." Piper leaned back in her chair and gently put her palms to her face. I fully expected tears of disbelief to fill her eyes, but she held her own. "I'm a good person. I am."

Of course, you are, my sweet Piper. He's the one dealing with all the inner turmoil.

"We know you are, Piper," I consoled, grateful when another table opened up that allowed Detective Jones to claim it for his talk with Heather. I noticed that Megan had decided to stay by Heather's side. Had Orwin not already cleared them for Cassie's murder, I would have said that was a sign of guilt. "Orwin, please tell me John Cooper recorded something on his phone that can help us."

We'll have to find a place to dispose of his skull.

By this time, Pearl had jumped up into Piper's lap. Her green eyes were fixated on me, as if she thought I would have the address of some secret place where we could dispose of the evidence.

"That is not how we deal with our cases," Orwin fiercely whispered, leaning forward to get his point across. Pearl had completely dumbfounded him, and there wasn't a thing I could do about it. I motioned for him to reply to my plea, thankful when he finally focused on the case. He lifted his phone to indicate he needed to do some more research. "I wish I could tell you that we had video proof of who killed Cassie Grier, but Cooper wasn't home. Give me five minutes to find out where he works, and then I'll pay him a visit. Do you think you can hold down the fort without the need for the fire department or the EMS?"

The two of you are clearly not seeing the danger you're allowing to brew up by ignoring the more important evidence in this mystery—Knox Emeric. He all but threatened my sweet Piper.

"Is there such a thing as a familiar mafia?"

Orwin had directed his question toward Piper, and I couldn't quite tell if he was trying to lighten the mood or if he was dead serious.

"Orwin, you're not going anywhere before you walk over to Knox Emeric and introduce yourself." I couldn't go another minute without knowing what the man knew and more importantly…whether or not he was of the supernatural realm. "Pearl has a point, though not about the evisceration thing. Knox is a complication, and we need to make sure he's not going to become a problem before we have a chance to solve this murder. On top of his involvement, we need to find out if Cassie Grier really did know about Piper's family."

Do you need spectacles? That…beast…already is a problem, and you're being distracted by his foul pheromones.

"Fine," Orwin mumbled, his stuffed-up nose clearly having gotten worse since he'd walked through the door to the café. "Anything to get away from crazytown over there."

"You don't mean that," Piper chided, giving Orwin a worried smile. "We enjoyed ourselves today. Pearl is just worried about me, and there are times that she overreacts. We can clear up this misunderstanding and then focus on Jamie. I'm confident that Cassie didn't know anything about me or my family. Our coven is very, very careful."

Or we can always use my method of cleaning up messes.

Piper had her head on straight, unlike Pearl. The longer we sat here, the more likely it was that an attempt on Jamie Lehman's life could take place. She was our sole mission right now, and Orwin could ease our worries within seconds. Besides, maybe Knox Emeric was simply some type of low-level warlock who somehow recognized our abilities and wanted to stir up trouble.

Knox Emeric is no warlock—no matter the level. I've told you this several times. You really should listen when someone is talking to you, dear.

I guess Pearl would know whether or not Knox was warlock, especially considering she could hear all thoughts of witches and warlocks in the magical realm. Unless, of course, Knox had used some type of warded spell to prevent familiars from doing so.

With that said, I do recall using my telekinesis at the back of the gas station when I couldn't find a bag of my favorite chips. I'd made sure that no one was around, but that wasn't always a guarantee with the advent of surveillance cameras. Maybe Knox really hadn't been sent here by Ammeline, and he was just fishing around for some evidence that all was not as it seemed.

Once again, Mr. Emeric is—

"Tad didn't kill Cassie Grier," Orwin exclaimed, leaning down and resting his hands on the table so that no one overheard him. He'd gotten up to walk across the café to get some insight into Knox, but such movement had put Orwin within six feet of Tad Whitaker. "Poor guy. He's having it rough today, but he's grateful for the mindless work of making drinks."

"See?" Piper said, resting her hand on my arm. "Tad had nothing to do with Cassie's death. Neither did Heather, Megan, or Vickie. And we've ruled out those three men who were standing in line with Orwin, so that only leaves…"

Pearl frowned, as well as both Orwin and myself.

What had we missed?

Quite a lot, it seems. It's simply process of elimination, leaving one Knox Emeric as the guilty party.

I was a full believer in process of elimination, but it was like we'd missed something that had been right in front of us all along.

I quietly turned in my chair for the first time since sitting down at the table Detective Jones had claimed earlier, taking the time to scan the faces of those at the numerous tables and booths.

Detective Jones was deep into his conversation with Heather and Megan.

"…discovered some things have happened lately, and all of these occurrences are connected to you, Ms. Coyle. The gentleman who interviewed you for the position at Cassie Grier's work was mugged three days ago. The property manager who didn't respond to your call regarding the leak underneath your bathroom sink reported a break-in at her office. The man living in the apartment above yours who you reported as being too loud had his sound system stolen last week. I'd say that being around you, Ms. Coyle, is bad luck at the minimum and hazardous to one's health at the extreme."

Where was Detective Jones leading this conversation? Orwin had already ruled out Heather Coyle as the killer. Why were so many crimes linked to Heather?

"Cassie was the one who got the job over Heather," Piper whispered, having overheard the detective make his case. "Could Orwin have missed something?"

No one's perfect, my darling.

"No, Orwin didn't miss anything."

I agreed with Pearl that no one was perfect. With that said, only someone who understood how Orwin's gift worked could have kept specific thoughts away from him. Heather? She was an intelligent woman, but she was merely human and didn't have the advantage of the magical realm behind her.

We needed to think outside the box.

We'd based the motive on someone hating Cassie enough to kill her, but what if her murder was based on what she'd done to Heather? From the way the detective laid out the summary of events, anyone who upset Heather had been punished.

Had Heather hired someone to do all those horrible things?

After giving that two seconds worth of thought, it wasn't unlikely.

Had Jamie done something to Heather?

Was that why the café manager was now a target?

Come to think of it, Jamie spilled a drink on Ms. Coyle the day of her interview a few weeks ago. You can imagine how that went over, but Jamie apologized profusely and even comped Heather's next few drink orders. Honestly, that was more than I would have done given her screeching that could have broken glass.

Tad was still behind the counter, calling out names of customers whose drink orders were ready. Jamie was speaking with the cashier, safe from harm.

For now. It never occurred to me that Mr. Emeric might believe he's some knight in shining armor. I guess there is a chance that he fancies himself in love with Ms. Coyle. Love has blinded many people over the years.

"I haven't seen Mr. Emeric around town before this entire thing started, so that's unlikely." Piper gently stroked Pearl's back as they continued their conversation, thankfully making it seem to everyone else that the blonde barista was talking to me. "Anyway, I overheard Heather say a while ago that she was thinking of dating some tech guy who lives in her apartment building, but that something held her back from saying yes. I can't quite recall her exact words, but I got the impression there was something off about the guy. I know this may come across as selfish, but I'm still worried over the fact that Mr. Emeric knows so much about me and my family…especially if he's just an everyday human."

Orwin was halfway across the café toward Knox in order to either confirm or deny the man's involvement with the crime—who currently made no pretense of watching me and my friends. There wasn't even a hint of panic in Knox's expression, which pretty much reassured me that he wasn't the murderer.

Fortunately, there were no longer any druids in the vicinity to get in the way of Orwin's gift. As I waited for Orwin to give me a signal on whether or not we'd cracked the case, I did one more perusal of the patrons.

Heather was currently adamantly denying anything to do with the crimes of those people who'd upset her, Megan was doing her best to defend her friend, Tad was still serving the customers, and Sophia and Emma were at a corner table talking to one another. Both the college girls were looking out the display window where Michael Pierce and his cameraman were walking down the sidewalk.

And behind them was one John Cooper—the single witness from last night none of us had been able to question.

Oh, I just had a zing of satisfaction! That was quite

exhilarating, if I do say so myself.

I'd call my zing a combination of concern and fear, but I did get what Pearl was hinting at—we might very well have solved the case.

Unfortunately, we now had a major problem on our hands.

Chapter Sixteen

"PIPER, WHAT DID you say about Heather dating someone from her apartment building?"

"I overheard Megan talking about it when she and Heather were in line the other day. She said something about the guy knowing things he shouldn't, and that he made her uncomfortable. Did I miss something? I'm not seeing the connection with Mr. Emeric."

Hold onto your hat, my sweet Piper. The adrenaline rush of solving a mystery is quite satisfying.

Piper was turned in her chair facing me, so she didn't pick up on what Pearl and I were seeing out the display window.

No time to explain. We must spring into action!

Pearl jumped down from Piper's lap as multiple things happened at once.

Orwin finally gave his signal, which was to slowly shake his head from side to side. He was now standing next to Knox to let me know that he wasn't the guilty party, though his arched brow told me he'd caught something of interest. Most likely it had to do with

Ammeline, but she and her minion would have to wait until I could secure Jamie Lehman's safety.

I had already put two and two together, but an algebra problem was staring me right in the face...and I didn't have time to go through all the steps to find the right answer.

No need for math, dear. Follow my lead.

Pearl had seen our tiny problem, as well.

Jamie...well, she was calling out to Tad that she'd forgotten her phone in her car and that she wouldn't be long. She was leaving the café, straight into the sights of John Cooper.

This was it.

I could practically picture the future events, but not in the same manner in which I was inflicted with a vision. No, this was my imagination stating clearly what would happen should we allow Jamie to leave the café.

The shift manager would walk to her vehicle, which she most likely parked in the lot down the road near the mall due to the fact that this place was so crowded, and she would be stabbed to death by none other than John Cooper for simply spilling a drink on the subject of his obsession.

John Cooper had allowed his fixation to escalate to the point where he needed to kill.

Well, don't just sit there. Make this look convincing, and whatever you do, do not make her squish me into a pancake.

"What is Pearl talking about?" Piper asked at a loss since she was only able to hear Pearl's side of the conversation.

Pearl and I didn't have time to answer.

The white feline dashed in front of Jamie, allowing me to flick my wrist and make it appear as if Jamie had tripped over Pearl. In reality, Jamie had already seen the cat and would have been able to avoid her had I not given her a bit of a nudge.

A bit of a nudge?

Pearl shook off where Jamie's foot had caught her in the side before gracefully rubbing herself on Jamie's shoulder. To any bystander, she was just a sweet white kitty who hadn't meant to cause a bit of mayhem.

I do believe the poor girl lost all the air in her lungs. Don't just sit there. Help her up and figure out how to let the good detective know that John Cooper is Cassie Grier's murderer.

"What?" Piper exclaimed in a fierce whisper as Detective Jones and Orwin both rushed to Jamie's side. "John Cooper? He..."

"He's definitely the one," I whispered in confirmation, quickly rising from my seat to make my way toward the exit. It didn't appear that John was coming into the café, but instead walking past to get a glimpse of Heather and avoid Detective Jones. In all likelihood, had Jamie walked outside alone, John would have taken the opportunity to hurt someone who he believed offended the woman he'd become obsessed with. "Stay here and make sure that Jamie is okay."

I *had* nudged the manager a bit harder than I'd intended, but I couldn't take the chance that Jamie would have brushed herself off and still walked out the door to her death. Before I did anything though, I needed that point zero one percent filled in for my own peace of mind.

"Heather." I stopped at her chair, blocking her view of the others attempting to help Jamie off of the floor. "Heather, look at me. Was John Cooper the man who asked you out last week?"

"What?" Heather tried to peer around me, but I shifted to keep her focus on me. "John? Yes, he was the one who asked me out last week. How did you—"

I barely felt the cool fall temperature as I barreled through the door, but it was a bit of a shock when the drizzling rain began to come down a little steadier. No wonder Michael Pierce and his cameraman had called it a day. They were entering the café as I'd busted out, but John Cooper continued to walk by the second display window with barely a glance.

What do you think you're doing, going off alone like that? This is why you need your own familiar—to keep you out of trouble. I wouldn't want that job for love nor money. You are quite the handful, you know.

I'd fallen into step behind our suspect, following him close enough to garner his attention but not enough for him to confront me. When I'd given Piper an order to stay behind, I'd meant for Pearl to do the same.

My dear, have you not heard the saying that a leopard cannot change its spots? Mr. Cooper will likely try and remove you as the obstinate obstacle you are, thereby unknowingly threatening to expose your extraordinary lineage to those human witnesses mulling about with their umbrellas. You and I both know you have the ability to eviscerate him…in the same manner I've reserved for Mr. Emeric.

"Pearl, I've done this a time or two," I muttered, shoving my hands in my black leather jacket. Gloves would have been nice, but I'd left them in the Jeep believing I wouldn't have need for them. I dodged around one of those navy-blue umbrellas Pearl had been talking about, grateful that some of the storefronts had those green awnings to prevent me from becoming saturated with rainwater. "And we are not eviscerating Knox, especially now that we know he wasn't responsible for Cassie Grier's death. We'll figure out how he knows about Piper later. Right now, you need to go back and make sure that Jamie is okay, and that Piper is doing her part."

I left Mr. Cornelia in charge, although I do doubt that boy's sanity from time to time.

Pearl hadn't made herself visible, although I could feel her next to me. I wasn't going to waste time arguing, especially when John Cooper quickly veered right and entered a rather thin alleyway in between two shops. By the time I turned the corner, he had vanished.

I must say that I think I'd rather prefer that zing of satisfaction at solving a mystery over the trepidation that someone could jump out at us with a really sharp knife. I'm not fond of being put in this situation, Miss Lilura. I've been on this plane of existence for over two thousand years, and I'd like to double that, if possible. Being around you seems to lessen my chances of that happening.

Larger drops of rain were now coming down steadily, and it was only a matter of time before the storm was right overhead. My black hair was now soaked into long strands, cold rivulets of water were running down the back of my neck and sneaking past the collar of my jacket, and I had to blink away tiny droplets of water that were hanging off my lashes.

None of that mattered.

John Cooper's surrender was all I could focus on. It was in times like this that my anger for being put into a situation where I was confronting a killer instead of being in front of a class full of freshman college students teaching what I loved came through like a strike of lightning.

Ammeline Letty Romilda was to blame, but these sick individuals who took lives as if they didn't matter were even worse. They needed to be stopped.

You're beginning to sound like you're going over the edge, darling. Orwin's obsession with little green men is about all the conspiracy theories I can take, so let's finish this murder mystery so that we can go about our lives, shall we?

With a flick of my wrist, I easily moved the large,

overfilled dumpster into the middle of the alleyway.

Nicely done, my dear!

Unfortunately, John Cooper hadn't been hiding behind the huge steel container as I'd thought he'd been.

I hate to admit it, but that was rather anticlimactic.

The only other hiding place available to John Cooper was the small indented doorway that held a side entrance into one of the shops. Without hesitation, I flicked my wrist once more, all but ensuring anything or anyone in the small alcove would be thrown out and laid at my feet.

"What the—"

A knife clattered on the wet asphalt, and John Cooper wasn't far behind. The weight of his backpack had him landing with a thud. Before the man could say another word, I'd moved the knife up and parallel with the ground and made sure the sharp blade hovered two feet from his chest.

Uh, Miss Lilura, don't you think you might be taking this a bit too far?

"Weren't you the one who suggested we eviscerate a certain someone not five minutes ago?" As usual, my anger receded just as quickly as it appeared. I didn't wait for Pearl to answer me, but instead continued to walk forward until I could kneel at eye level with the knife.

Oh, my. You do make quite the adversary.

"Mr. Cooper, I'm only going to ask you this once." I waited patiently for John to meet my gaze, though he was quite reluctant to look away from the sharp weapon hanging in midair and pointed in his direction. "Did you kill Cassie Grier?"

Remind me never to have you interrogate me, Miss Lilura.

"Who are you? How are you doing that?" John exclaimed in abstract horror as he scrambled back from the knife. I continued to move it forward, showing him there was no way out. "Stop! Just…fine, alright? I killed Cassie, but what she did to my Heather was wrong!"

I can see why that confession didn't take long. We might need to talk about the way you conduct your so-called debriefings before you drive out of town. I wouldn't want it to be said that I didn't give you the benefit of some sound advice. I do have my rather stellar reputation to uphold.

"W-what are you?" John asked in a tone that was barely coming out as a whisper. He was clearly freaking out and not accepting what he was seeing with his own two eyes. "How are you d-doing that?"

John was more concerned about who and what I was than anything else, but it didn't matter. He'd committed murder, and it was time he pay for his crimes. I purposefully took my time standing there before advancing toward the broken man lying on the sidewalk, ensuring that the knife followed me until I was close enough to make sure he heard every word I said…and would follow my orders.

It's good to know that you take our need for secrecy seriously, Miss Lilura.

"Listen to me very closely, Mr. Cooper. You are

going to do exactly what I say, and you will never mention this to anyone. Trust me when I say you don't want to know what will happen if you ever utter a single word of what occurred in this alleyway today."

Very well done, my dear. Very well done. I mean, you didn't need to sound as if you're in the mafia that Mr. Cornelia spoke of, but that's neither here nor there. I shouldn't nitpick how you do your job. Now, I'd say we both deserve a spot of tea after such a busy morning, don't you?

Chapter Seventeen

"I THINK THAT'S everything," Orwin said, slamming the back of the Jeep closed with a satisfying thud. "We managed to get one more checkmark in the win column, seeing as we saved Jamie Lehman before your vision came true. I'd call that a par, given that we fell short on our primary objective."

It certainly was a win for Jamie, but as far as I was concerned, we were still on the losing end of that tally if one combined all of our cases we'd worked over the last three months. It also didn't help that Knox Emeric had skipped town before we could find out if there was any truth to what he'd said about Cassie knowing the Allifair family's secret.

"You always have to rain on my celebration, don't you?" Orwin mumbled, having picked up my thoughts as if I'd spoken them aloud. "Did you manage to at least get us a late checkout from the motel manager?"

I nodded my answer before checking the time on my cell phone. It was a little after eight o'clock at night. The storms had moved out of the area, leaving that damp chill in the air that for some reason had settled deep into my bones. It was an abysmal weariness that didn't want to fade.

It might have to do with the fact that Heather Coyle had found out how close to death she had come, especially in light of John Cooper's confession. True to his word—not that he'd had any real choice of the matter—he'd gotten up off the wet asphalt in the alleyway and made his way back to the café, where he'd confessed to the murder of Cassie Grier.

Michael Pierce had gotten his exclusive clip of the reluctant admission, Detective Jones had made his arrest, and I figured Heather might have to go into therapy for some trust issues after what had happened today.

After her initial shock, disbelief, and anger that John Cooper had used her as an excuse to kill Cassie and harm others, she'd made it known how horrified she was at the thought—which had prompted John Cooper to lunge at her as if he'd lost what tenuous hold he had on his sanity. The only thing that had saved her from harm was the fact that he'd already been in cuffs. Detective Jones had controlled the situation with ease by yanking backward on the chain between the cuffs, and he eventually escorted John Cooper out of the café to what would hopefully be a life sentence in prison.

"Orwin, what did you find out when you got close enough to Knox Emeric to read his thoughts?" I asked, opening the driver's side door to the Jeep. Although

Orwin was right that we'd had a win today, something still wasn't setting well with me. "We never got a chance to talk about him, other than you saying he wasn't a threat to Piper or her family. How can you be so sure?"

I set my phone in the console, taking the time to remove my black leather jacket. It was always more comfortable for me to drive without the restriction of added layers. Orwin stayed on my side of the vehicle while I went through my routine of opening the back door and laying my jacket over a stack of books that he liked to have within arm's reach.

"Knox left the café the moment John Cooper confessed, but he'd definitely made a conscious decision of leaving things alone." Orwin seemed to hesitate before adding in his two cents. He even waited to say anything on the subject until he'd closed the back door and rested his shoulder against the frame of the Jeep. "I can only assume that he's got some ability to cloak his thoughts courtesy of the supernatural realm. He isn't entirely human, but he isn't a warlock, either. He knows who we are, which is how he was most likely able to steer his thoughts to meaningless things whenever I was within his vicinity."

"I don't like it."

I also didn't like that Knox Emeric had just simply vanished into thin air. We'd even taken a drive around town to make sure the Land Rover wasn't parked in some odd place that could potentially mean he was here to stay, thus causing Piper and her family trouble that they hadn't asked for.

"There's not much we can do about it, Lou." Orwin shrugged before taking his glasses off and cleaning them with his sweatshirt. He'd already stored his jacket in the back, along with his overnight bag. We'd be in Kecksburg soon, although I was still trying to figure a way out of that little side trip. "Don't even think about it. We need to take a break anyway to research the witch who lives in Minnesota. There was a video posted on social media showing her holding a séance as a prank on a friend, but I know what I saw…and that woman has some level of true ability to speak with her ancestors."

If that was the case, there could be someone on the other side who could help me in my quest to either find Ammeline or break this curse. That was a road trip we just couldn't pass up.

"Do we still have the metal detector?" Orwin asked after having repositioned his glasses on the bridge of his nose. "I want to take a few hours at the UFO crash site to see if we can get some concrete proof that it wasn't a satellite like those reports stated…you know, the same reports that were lost to a fire in the 1990s."

I reminded myself that Orwin put up with a lot on this quest, and the least I could give him was a bit of personal time to enjoy his bizarre hobby. Who was I to get in the way of his conspiracy theories and those UFOs?

"I can still hear you," Orwin replied wryly as he turned on the heel of his brown loafers to go digging in the back of the Jeep to ensure we had his metal detector. "It's getting pretty cold out here. You said you're driving first shift, so go ahead and climb in. I know the detector is in here somewhere."

It was a wonder we could find anything in the back of the Jeep with the way it was crammed with books, equipment, luggage, and the list went on. Even with leaving Piper and Pearl behind in the safety of Bedford, Pennsylvania, I'd made the decision to spend three quarters of my trust fund on the RV I'd been wanting to invest in. The company had offered to transport it to the closest major freight office as part of the closing, which was located in Pittsburgh. I'd drive there once Orwin was settled in Kecksburg. It only made sense, but we'd most likely have to watch every penny from this point on.

The mere thought of leaving Piper and Pearl behind was now stuck in my mind.

As I got comfortable behind the steering wheel, even starting the engine so that we could have some heat, a part of me had truly thought this trip would have ended differently. We hadn't needed the use of Piper's gift this trip, but I had no doubt that there would come a time when we would. She was a gem in the rough, and I had no doubt that she would leave her mark on the world.

And Pearl? Well, that sleek white familiar was an untapped source of vital information that could probably have led me straight to Ammeline's doorstep. Her vast reservoir of knowledge had seemed practically endless, but she belonged here with Piper.

"Don't forget that the dander from the Egyptian cotton ball would have been the death of me," Orwin interjected, having shut the back of the Jeep and climbed into the passenger seat. He had his laptop and headphones in hand. He inhaled deeply with ease and a lopsided smile. "See? Clear as a bell."

"Are you sure you don't want Piper to take care of that allergy problem for you before we leave town?" We'd discussed it thoroughly, but I still thought Orwin was being paranoid by refusing to lift the blocking spell he'd performed on himself against Ammeline. I understood that some of the components he needed to recreate the evocation might take a few months to gather, but we hadn't seen Ammeline since that fateful day. "Last chance."

I grabbed one of my hair ties and gathered up the long strands to keep them off my shoulders while driving. It never ended up looking like those cute messy buns seen on television, but at least I could drive with that small distraction out of the way.

"Oh, no," Orwin protested rather profusely, confusing me as to if he was reinstating his denial of Piper's help or warning me that my version of a messy bun had me looking as if I'd just survived sticking my finger into an electrical socket. "No. Absolutely not. We had this settled. Lou, don't you dare give in."

Settled?

Give in?

"Orwin, what in the world are you talking about?" I asked, completely lost in this conversation.

Had he picked up on some thoughts that hadn't even made their way to my consciousness? I'd learned early on never to rule anything out when it came to his gift.

"Curse," Orwin muttered, pinching the bridge of his nose the way he did when he was frustrated. "I think I'm as cursed as you are."

The flash of headlights pulling into the parking lot alerted me to the fact that Orwin hadn't been talking about me or his ability.

Piper expertly navigated her Prius into the slot next to mine with a big smile on her face. Pearl was in the passenger seat appearing to be meowing at the top of her lungs. She was most likely giving a lecture about long, drawn-out goodbyes…which we'd already exchanged.

"I don't think they're here to say goodbye." Orwin set his headphones on top of his laptop, sighing in resignation. "You and I both know Piper isn't cut out for this. We're basically gypsies with no place to call home on a quest to bring down a Lich queen. Piper is just too…"

"Innocent," I murmured, in full agreement with Orwin. "We can't just drive off without hearing what she has to say, though."

"I categorically and adamantly disagree." Orwin pushed up his glasses as Piper opened her car door, frowning at something that Pearl was probably shouting at this point. "We really, really ought to drive off. I mean, we'll give them a wave and all, but it would be in our best interest to leave right this second."

I wasn't going to lie. There was a part of me that wanted to hear Piper say she'd changed her mind about joining us. I could teach her what she needed to know. After all, I'd had the three-month crash course in solving Scooby Doo mysteries. Why couldn't she?

"You don't really want—"

I'd already opened the driver's side door, wincing when the cold wind blew inside. I didn't allow the damp chilliness or Orwin's loud protest to keep from exiting the Jeep.

"Piper, is everything okay?" I asked, meeting her halfway at the back of our parked vehicles. Pearl used her ability to materialize on the trunk of the car, her whiskers a little askew. "Pearl, not even when we were dealing with John Cooper did you seem so out of sorts. What's wrong? Has something else happened?"

"We're coming with you!"

Now is when I expect you to talk some sense into her, Miss Lilura.

I remained silent, digesting this news without showing any outward emotions. The right thing to do would be to tell Piper and Pearl that this wasn't a good idea.

Piper was too trusting and naïve, and Pearl was...well, Pearl.

Then do the right thing, my dear hexed one. Tell my sweet Piper that she must stay here in the safety net of her coven.

"Lou," Orwin warned, joining us while keeping his distance from Pearl. "Think about what you're doing."

"This is the right thing," Piper exclaimed, shaking her head at all three of us in disappointment. "Shame on all of you. Pearl, you said it yourself that Lou and Orwin are on a dangerous path and needed all the help they can get. We can be the ones to help them."

I was speaking about their mental health, my sweet Piper...not that we should join them.

"For once, I agree with the mangy feline." Orwin frowned when Pearl directed a short hiss in his direction. "What? I'm agreeing with you. My mental health can't deal with you on a daily basis. Look, we'll come to visit you the next time we're out this way. Okay?"

"Lou, you came here specifically so that I could heal you," Piper continued as if Pearl and Orwin hadn't said a word. "I can't do that, but even Orwin mentioned that having me with you in order to help others would be a benefit to your cause. Well, here I am. Cassie's murder not only changed a lot of lives here in Bedford, but her death opened my eyes, too. Yes, I could stay with my coven and take my time in learning the ways of my craft, but I could also join you and Orwin on this adventure of a lifetime by helping you save the people you see dying in your visions."

"You did say that," I muttered out of the side of my mouth, reminding Orwin that he'd once thought it was a good idea to have them join us.

"That was when I thought there was only one," Orwin corrected in dismay, holding up his right hand in surrender when it looked as if Pearl might lunge at him. "Let's just agree that we rub each other the wrong way. After all, your dander could literally kill me."

Don't tempt me.

Pearl settled back down on her haunches after having the last word, all of us knowing she truly wouldn't do such a thing. At least, I don't think she would resort to those extremes.

Another gust of wind came through, all but warning us another storm was brewing. I wrapped my arms around my waist, needing to make a decision.

Please don't remind me that I could be at home near a warm fire after having a spot of cream brewed up to just the right temperature. Piper, my sweet, you need to listen to reason. You—

"Pearl, you taught me that this gift I've been given can help humanity as a whole." Piper spoke gently, stepping forward until she rested what must be very cold fingers on the trunk of her car. "Imagine all of the people we can save if we do this together. You're always saying that fate puts obstacles, choices, and gifts in our paths. Well, this is all three. You know this is the right thing to do, and I need you by my side."

Well, when you put it like that…

"Please tell me that you have enough money to cover that RV we've been talking about." It appeared that Orwin could see where Piper and Pearl's conversation was heading, because after that little speech, I wasn't going to turn down the help. We'd been lucky that some of the mysteries we'd solved over the last three months had been relatively uncomplicated, but they wouldn't always be like that. "And I want my own desk with shelves, an unlimited wireless hotspot plan, and a high-end desktop we can use as a server. I'm going to need something to take my mind off the fact that I can't breathe."

Seeing as you're taking requests, I'll need a spot by a window that allows sunshine to come through the majority of the day. You'll also need to supply me with my nightcap of creamer, warmed to just the right temperature. Piper will give you a list of my special dietary needs.

"Piper, are you sure about this?" I asked, needing to know for myself that this was truly something she wanted to do instead of staying with her family, friends, and coven. "What about your parents? Have you—"

"I didn't work my shift today," Piper shared as she tucked her blonde hair behind her ear when a breeze tried to blow some strands into her heart-shaped face. "Instead, I handed in my notice and went home to have a very long and serious discussion with my parents. Honestly, they're the reason I'm so late. They understand and finally accept that this is something I need to do for myself. We cannot allow Ammeline Letty Romilda to continue this madness of cursing her fellow witches."

You realize that my sweet girl is leaving out the part where her father almost had a heart attack.

"He did not," Piper countered with a frown. "I promised to call them as much as I can to give them updates. They also gave me my great-great grandfather's notes on the first coven and those specifically regarding the Allifair lineage. Maybe there's something in his journals that refers to hexes such as yours."

I could only hope that was the case. Knowing that I sometimes jumped headfirst into situations, I counted to ten. The pros far outweighed the cons, especially knowing that Pearl would be around to make sure that Piper remained safe if we ended up dealing with more druids, a nest of vampires, or a pack of wolves. It would also be nice to have somewhat of a guarantee that Orwin survived this dangerous quest, because there were times I had my doubts. Piper had the ability to make sure he came away unscathed.

Eventually, I slowly let my inhalation expel through my lips and gave my nod of consent.

Piper picked up Pearl and drew her into an embrace, which the white feline seemed to acquiesce to with adoration. I'd never seen her so affectionate, and it just affirmed my choice that we could all keep Piper safe while she did the same for us in general...and someday maybe even help me with my curse.

As for Orwin, he didn't say a word about my decision.

Seriously, not one word.

He just simply opened up the back of the Jeep and began searching through his things. Piper and I shared a concerned look as Pearl gave what almost resembled a satisfied smile. Her ability to read our thoughts would take some getting used to, but at least I'd be able to count on her to tell me if something were really wrong with either of my traveling companions.

"Orwin, what are you doing?"

"What does it look like I'm doing?" Orwin finally came up with an empty over-the-counter medicine bottle. "It figures."

"The RV will have plenty of room for each of you to have your own space." There was no point in leaving Bedford tonight when we wouldn't be able to take both vehicles. I fully intended to hook the Jeep onto the back of the RV, but Piper's parents should keep the Prius. "Looks like we're spending one more night in Bedford."

It appears that your little flying saucers will have to wait, alien hunter.

"You keep that up, and I'll personally give you a one-way ticket to a space—"

"Let's start off on the right foot, shall we?" I prompted, sharing a smile with Piper.

It wasn't so bad to mix things up, was it?

At least you can cross werewolves off Piper's list of creatures to encounter. Now, vampires are another matter altogether. I confronted some of those bloodsuckers back in my Cleopatra days, but there's not so many around these parts. There has been a poltergeist or two, but they…

Pearl continued to talk about the various supernatural beings that Piper had yet to meet. It was evident that the white familiar was going to be a wealth of information, maybe even more so than Orwin's magical tomes, but something wasn't quite adding up.

"Pearl, what do you mean Piper's already dealt with a werewolf?"

I didn't realize I needed to spell it out for you, dear. Do you not recall that I referred to your Knox Emeric as the big bad wolf? I meant that quite literally. I've known Mr. Emeric was a werewolf from the very first sniff. That powerful wet dog odor is rather hard to miss.

"So that's what he was," Orwin murmured in acknowledgement, as if it all made sense. Well, it didn't. I had many questions that had been left unanswered, but something told me we hadn't seen the last of Knox Emeric. "I want you to know that I would have figured out what Emeric was had I been given enough time."

Pearl gave what looked to be another mollified smile as she swayed her tail behind her, still soaking in Piper's affection.

"What can I say?" Piper quipped with a grin and a small shrug. "Pearl likes it when she's right."

I had not one, but two know-it-alls who weren't able

to communicate properly.

"I resent being compared to a cat," Orwin muttered, tossing me the keys to the Jeep without once looking away from our new passengers. "You realize that I'm going to need to stock up on allergy medicine before we leave town, right?"

~ THE END ~

Thank you for reading the first book in the *Hex on Me Mysteries*! The gang is back for another mystery in *Cursing Up the Wrong Tree*, so please click below to grab your copy!

kennedylayne.com/cursing-up-the-wrong-tree.html

Witches, warlocks, and werewolves, oh my! Things get rather hairy in the next installment of the Hex on Me Mysteries by USA Today Bestselling Author Kennedy Layne…

Lou and the gang start out with every intention of tracking down a medium who they hope can speak to her ancestors and gain vital information in an effort to break the hex cast about by the only known immortal Lich Queen. They should have known their trip wouldn't quite go as planned.

Another vision that Lou has been cursed with comes to fruition, this time in the wilds of the Wyoming back country. What was the victim doing miles from civilization without adequate supplies? Residents in the neighboring town knows more than they're saying, yet all the evidence points in a different direction.

Things are about to come to a head under the light of the full moon. You'll need to make sure you have a bit of silver in your pocket before joining Lou and the others for another mystifying whodunit…this one promises to have fangs!

BOOKS BY KENNEDY LAYNE

HEX ON ME MYSTERIES
If the Curse Fits
Cursing Up the Wrong Tree

PARAMOUR BAY MYSTERIES
Magical Blend
Bewitching Blend
Enchanting Blend
Haunting Blend
Charming Blend
Spellbinding Blend
Cryptic Blend

OFFICE ROULETTE SERIES
Means (Office Roulette, Book One)
Motive (Office Roulette, Book Two)
Opportunity (Office Roulette, Book Three)

KEYS TO LOVE SERIES
Unlocking Fear (Keys to Love, Book One)
Unlocking Secrets (Keys to Love, Book Two)
Unlocking Lies (Keys to Love, Book Three)
Unlocking Shadows (Keys to Love, Book Four)
Unlocking Darkness (Keys to Love, Book Five)

SURVIVING ASHES SERIES
Essential Beginnings (Surviving Ashes, Book One)
Hidden Ashes (Surviving Ashes, Book Two)
Buried Flames (Surviving Ashes, Book Three)

Endless Flames (Surviving Ashes, Book Four)
Rising Flames (Surviving Ashes, Book Five)

CSA CASE FILES SERIES
Captured Innocence (CSA Case Files 1)
Sinful Resurrection (CSA Case Files 2)
Renewed Faith (CSA Case Files 3)
Campaign of Desire (CSA Case Files 4)
Internal Temptation (CSA Case Files 5)
Radiant Surrender (CSA Case Files 6)
Redeem My Heart (CSA Case Files 7)
A Mission of Love (CSA Case Files 8)

RED STARR SERIES
Starr's Awakening(Red Starr, Book One)
Hearths of Fire (Red Starr, Book Two)
Targets Entangled (Red Starr, Book Three)
Igniting Passion (Red Starr, Book Four)
Untold Devotion (Red Starr, Book Five)
Fulfilling Promises (Red Starr, Book Six)
Fated Identity (Red Starr, Book Seven)
Red's Salvation (Red Starr, Book Eight)

THE SAFEGUARD SERIES
Brutal Obsession (The Safeguard Series, Book One)
Faithful Addiction (The Safeguard Series, Book Two)
Distant Illusions (The Safeguard Series, Book Three)
Casual Impressions (The Safeguard Series, Book Four)
Honest Intentions (The Safeguard Series, Book Five)
Deadly Premonitions (The Safeguard Series, Book Six)

About the Author

First and foremost, I love life. I love that I'm a wife, mother, daughter, sister… and a writer.

I am one of the lucky women in this world who gets to do what makes them happy. As long as I have a cup of coffee (maybe two or three) and my laptop, the stories evolve themselves and I try to do them justice. I draw my inspiration from a retired Marine Master Sergeant that swept me off of my feet and has drawn me into a world that fulfills all of my deepest and darkest desires. Erotic romance, military men, intrigue, with a little bit of kinky chili pepper (his recipe), fill my head and there is nothing more satisfying than making the hero and heroine fulfill their destinies.

Thank you for having joined me on their journeys…

Email: kennedylayneauthor@gmail.com

Facebook: facebook.com/kennedy.layne.94

Twitter: twitter.com/KennedyL_Author

Website: www.kennedylayne.com

Newsletter:
www.kennedylayne.com/aboutnewsletter.html

www.ingramcontent.com/pod-product-compliance
Lightning Source LLC
Chambersburg PA
CBHW071512170626
46811CB00007B/2831